MEMENTO MORI

MEMENTO MORI

a novel

EUNICE HONG

Red Hen Press | *Pasadena, CA*

Book design by Mark E. Cull.

Library of Congress Cataloging-in-Publication Data

Names: Hong, Eunice, 1989– author.
Title: Memento mori / Eunice Hong.
Description: First edition. | Pasadena, CA: Red Hen Press, 2024.
Identifiers: LCCN 2024001589 (print) | LCCN 2024001590 (ebook) | ISBN
  9781636281872 (paperback) | ISBN 9781636281889 (ebook)
Subjects: LCGFT: Novels.
Classification: LCC PS3608.O49444 M46 2024 (print) | LCC PS3608.O49444
  (ebook) | DDC 813/.6—dc23/eng/20240116
LC record available at https://lccn.loc.gov/2024001589
LC ebook record available at https://lccn.loc.gov/2024001590

The National Endowment for the Arts, the Los Angeles County Arts Commission, the Ahmanson Foundation, the Dwight Stuart Youth Fund, the Max Factor Family Foundation, the Pasadena Tournament of Roses Foundation, the Pasadena Arts & Culture Commission and the City of Pasadena Cultural Affairs Division, the City of Los Angeles Department of Cultural Affairs, the Audrey & Sydney Irmas Charitable Foundation, the Meta & George Rosenberg Foundation, the Albert and Elaine Borchard Foundation, the Adams Family Foundation, Amazon Literary Partnership, the Sam Francis Foundation, and the Mara W. Breech Foundation partially support Red Hen Press.

First Edition
Published by Red Hen Press
www.redhen.org

To A.
and
To everyone who set me on my way

MEMENTO MORI

Sing, muse
of grief.

Is there a muse of grief?

Once upon a time . . .

the goddess of the grain had a joyful, fair-haired daughter who liked to wander and dance in her mother's emerald fields. One shining day, as lightning streaked across the bronze sky, a bolt hit the earth and exploded into a riot of flowers for the girl—roses of crimson and snow, pink-blue hyacinths, milky white narcissuses with blood-red hearts. The girl thought her mother and father had sent her these flowers, and she delighted in them.

So taken was the girl with the godlike hues and shapes bursting from the earth that she did not see their stems slowly creeping higher and higher. As she turned back to return to her mother, she was faced with a dense undergrowth. The roses she had admired now menaced her with sharp thorns above her head. A thick tendril of ivy curled around her slender ankles and rooted her in place. She knew then that this could not be her mother, and she cried out. But her voice was stifled by the violet and cream petals that grew large and swooped over her in an opaque canopy that blotted out the sun.

And she was afraid.

She heard behind her the muffled sound of hooves. A dark shadow reached out to her, and she tried to run. She desperately twisted her ankles this way and that to rend herself from the ivy. Her right foot broke free, but the hooves galloped ever closer. Her left foot broke free and she moved to run through the thorns, though she knew they would tear her face and hands and hair. But before she could throw herself into the brambles, she felt the shadow grasp her around the waist and pull her into a chariot so dark that it seemed to swallow light itself.

Hearing in the distance the rumble of thunder and the cry of an eagle, she breathed, believing her father had come to rescue her. But no one came. The earth opened up and swallowed the dark chariot, with her in it.

Who had carried her away but the Unseen One himself?

"Which one is the Unseen One?"

Hades, god of the underworld. The girl found herself in the wide-gated house below. The shadow pulled her into his chambers and took her, unwilling.

"Took her where? ... Oh."

Yes. Oh. Afterward, he led her into a vast chamber with an oval table of glassy obsidian in its center, ringed by fireplaces flickering with dark flames that cast a pale gray light. And he motioned for her to sit down. She, still unwilling, sat.

A cup of deep ruby wine appeared before her. But she would not drink. Then there appeared before her a platter of hammered silver with the choicest cut of a young calf, roasted and seasoned with holy salt. She turned away. Next came a loaf of golden-brown bread, freshly baked. The shadow broke the loaf in half and showed her the chestnuts and walnuts studded inside. He offered her the bread with steam still rising from its soft center, but she forced her hands to stay by her side. Then came a rich, warm soup of spiced squash and cream. This, too, she refused. He left her alone in the chamber, and food continued to appear before her: savory oxtail stew, seared fish encrusted with nuts and seeds, silky egg custard, plump black grapes, golden sweetcakes, roasted brown eels. But nothing passed her lips. A crystal glass of honey nectar appeared before her and faded away, undrunk. Wheels of soft, ripe cheese rolled away, never unwrapped. Salty green olives went untasted. Juicy figs dangled before her, only to wither, unchosen.

"I'm hungry."

After an eternity, the Unseen One returned.

"Have you eaten?"

These were the first words he had spoken to her since he had taken her from the sunshine. She shook her head but said nothing. He took her again, still unwilling, to his chambers. She stayed on the bed in tears, wishing for her mother, until she fell into a dreamless sleep.

She awoke to a sudden flash of sickly yellow light. She bolted upright, but the shadow left her there and did not return. Spent from crying and curiosity, she fell back into an uneasy sleep. She was gently shaken awake by a laughing-eyed boy with shining hair and a golden staff in his hand. On his feet, he wore dark leather sandals with golden straps and crystal wings. The brilliance of him against the gray gloom seared her eyes.

He bowed to her. "Queen, I am sent by your mother, who blesses the earth, and your father, who gathers the clouds."

She jumped up. "You have come to bring me home."

"I have come to find you, to see that you are well. My only task now is to bring a message back to your mother. This is your home now."

She shook her head in disbelief. "It is not my home. I was taken, unwilling."

"Why did you not cry out?"

"I did! He stilled my voice."

"Why did you not struggle?"

"I did! He overpowered me."

"Why did you not refuse him?"

"I did! But he took me, unwilling."

She was weeping now, shimmering tears streaming from her bright eyes.

The laughing-eyed boy twirled his staff carelessly, and it seemed to writhe in the light of the dark fire.

"You must speak with your husband."

"He is not—" She stopped, seeing that her words were futile. She stood slowly and found the great shadow at the obsidian table. She sat beside him and steeled herself to speak, but he spoke first. "I will send you back up to your mother with the messenger."

She jumped up, and he held up a hand. "But then you will return to me."

She said nothing.

"When you return, you will have half my realm and your power will equal mine, and you will never want for anything. Do you accept these terms?"

He took her right wrist with his hand, and she willed herself not to shrink back. She looked up at him but said nothing.

He smiled at her. "You have not eaten or drunk since you arrived." He held out a bright pomegranate that glowed in the light of the dark fire. In his left hand, he offered a razor edge of obsidian.

She was so thirsty and the shadow had offered her no water. Taking the glinting blade, she cut into the round flesh of the orb and broke apart the two halves, tearing away the creamy white membrane. Nestled within was a cluster of translucent, shimmering jewels, the plumpest seeds she had ever seen. She was so thirsty. She plucked out a garnet seed and slowly, carefully, placed it in her mouth.

She bit into a burst of sunshine and began to cry, thinking of her mother's fields. She plucked another seed.

And another.

And another.

And another.

And another.

The laughing-eyed boy came to her then. Taking her by the hand, he wrapped her in a yellow mist. When it fell away, she saw her beloved mother lying on the barren ground, forehead to the earth. Everything that grew from the soil had burned away in the fire of her mother's rage, and the waters and skies had frozen still in the shade of her mother's grief.

She reached out to touch her mother's lovely hair, and the goddess of the grain, looking up, reached back to her in disbelief and wonder. They rejoiced, and the laughing-eyed boy flew off. The daughter told her mother all that had happened, and together, they lamented.

But she did not tell her mother about the pomegranate seeds.

The earth again grew abundant with delicate flowers and golden wheat and hardy olives—everywhere except for the place where the daughter had been taken. Nothing grew there but a ring of black poplars, and the ground within turned to ash and salt. The daughter never left her bountiful mother's side, and each day that the Unseen One did not appear before her, the tight grip on her chest loosened.

"If he's Unseen, obviously he won't appear before her, DUH."

Very astute, thank you. One evening, as rose and violet streaked the sky and the sun headed down past the horizon, the daughter rested her head comfortably on her mother's shoulder while they watched the stars emerge. And suddenly, from far away and then right behind her, she heard a bleat and a roar. The sky lit up and she saw the laughing-eyed boy driving a pair of winged lions toward them while herding a flock of goats.

And she grew afraid.

Her earth-nourishing mother, suspecting nothing, petted the lions and murmured soft words to them.

"I want a pet lion! I'm going to dress Lilly up as a lion for Halloween."

I think the pet store sells those soft cones for dogs in the shape of a lion's mane. We can get one, it'll be funny. Now hush, you're supposed to be falling asleep.

"Almost sleepy. What happened next?"

The laughing-eyed boy spoke. "The one below sends for his Queen."

And the fair-haired mother grew a hundredfold. Her voice became terrible and cold. "He will not take her again."

"But the Queen has agreed."

The daughter tried to hide her face from her mother, but there was nowhere to turn.

"Daughter, did you accept anything he offered you?"

"I accepted nothing freely."

The laughing-eyed boy spoke softly, without laughter. "Why then, Queen, does your body betray you?"

And she cried out. From her stomach crept forth six golden threads. Two strands wound down her legs and clasped her slender ankles. Two more twirled down her arms and bound her wrists. She tore frantically at the fifth thread wrapping around her neck, to no avail—she felt it close firmly around her throat, though it did not choke her. She arched her head back as she felt the last thread crawl around her waist and up her spine to circle her lovely hair. She looked at her wrists in despair. Each circlet of gold was clasped shut by a single garnet.

The laughing-eyed boy knelt before her, and her mother shrank down to earth. "I have no power to save you now, daughter."

"Please, mother. Please. Please don't make me go."

The goddess of the grain did not speak, but the ground began to wither and turn to ash. The Queen—for that's what she had become—could not lift her head for weeping. She dropped to the ground and threw her hands around her mother's knees in supplication, but her fingers passed right through them. The laughing-eyed boy picked her up and laid her gently on the back of a lion. He mounted the other and they descended, leaving her mother with the goats.

The one below awaited her. Clasping her right wrist, he led her into his chambers. "Queen. You have returned."

She did not speak, and she did not look at him.

"You have half this realm and your power equals mine and you will never want for anything."

She said nothing.

"If you would only speak, Queen, and move my heart."

And so she spoke. "For six seeds, I am bound to you, unwilling, in this hateful place."

"You took freely what I offered."

"You deceived me. I had no choice." His silence made her scream. "My mother will desolate the earth. She will scorch the ground and choke the air. Nothing will grow. And when my father realizes that there is no one left to sacrifice to him, he who gathers the clouds will regret the day he flew by your chariot and gave me to you."

For she had realized it was her father who had gifted her away.

The Unseen One said nothing. She continued, her voice ringing. "And you will rule nothing. This realm will never grow. No one new will come. There will be nothing but the same day for time without end and you will languish, deathless, forever."

"I cannot release you."

                              "Well, not with THAT attitude."

She wrenched her arm out of his hand and tore desperately, again, at the circlets binding her slender ankles, her pale wrists, her long neck, her lovely hair. But they held fast.

At last, she spoke again. "But you can send me back up to my mother for part of the year, as you have done. And the messenger will bear me back. For he is ever on time." Her voice was bitter.

The Unseen One said nothing, but nodded.

"Swear. Swear on the Styx."

"I swear on the Styx."

> "Sticks? Why does he have to swear it on
> sticks? Like did he have sticks up his—"

Not sticks. The River Styx. Gods who swore oaths on the River Styx were bound by their word, or else they would be banished from divinity for nine years.

And so it was. For part of each year, the Queen returned to her mother, and the goddess and the earth rejoiced with the girl.

And for part of each year, the goddess above grew still in rage and grief, and the earth became barren.

> "And that's why we have snow days."

Perhaps. An alternate explanation is that this might be why we have summer. In some of the places this story was told, the summer heat would have killed the crops, but the mild fall and winter would have been perfect for growing and harvest.

Now lie back down, you're supposed to be going to sleep.

The Queen below remained icy, still, unwilling. And her heart grew as barren as the earth above her. She gazed at the smoky river that wound through the realm and wondered if she, too, could drink from its waters and forget all that came before. She sat by the golden pool of memory and saw the mighty souls of heroes lying content and boastful in a bright glen guarded by dark forms.

She watched without seeing the multitudes of shades arriving at her kingdom's shores, newly shed of their mortal bodies. She heard, without listening, their cries to be returned above. But plenty of shades, she noticed, did not ask to return. She envied and pitied these shades the most—and above all, a young woman who arrived crowned in the pet-aled garland of a bride. She came ashore without complaint, neither be-fuddled nor distressed like so many others.

The Queen found herself observing the bride. Would she drink the wa-ters of the smoky river and forget her past, sorrow and joy alike, to be born anew? Or seek instead the golden pool of memory and its bright knowledge?

"Is this place a water park or something?"

There does seem to be a lot of water in the underworld. The bride chose neither the smoky river nor the golden pool. The Queen watched her wander for days through the fields of asphodel, perhaps delighting in her freedom from the shackles of the body and who knows what else. Or perhaps she was searching for someone. And the Queen yearned for her mother's fields and wondered when the laughing-eyed boy would come.

One day, long after the bride had arrived, a man with a silver lyre ap-peared. A whole man, with his body intact. The Unseen One trembled in rage, and the Queen took her throne beside him to soothe his quak-ing. It was only a mortal man, after all. A throng of shades grew thick behind the man, curious, longing for life and breath and blood.

The Unseen One gripped the Queen's left arm, just above her golden fet-ter, as he roared at the man.

"How dare you?"

The man did not flinch, but bowed to them and plucked his lyre. As he began to sing, the shifting air stilled and the unending rivers lulled. In the distance, the young girl sank to her knees in the asphodel by the smoky river, and the Queen, ever watchful, knew that the man had come for her.

When the last note faded into silence, the Queen saw that the shades wept. Even the Unseen One's voice softened, though his grip did not, as he turned his gaze to the Queen.

"What would you have me do?"

**I, being of unsound mind and body,
devise and bequeath my property
both real and unreal, as follows:**

To you, my brother, M.: These pages of me, of us, of our family. My hope is that you continue to be the merry boy you have always been, and that you remember me as your heroine and not just your impatient older sister.

To my friend, K.: All of my headphones. (You may think, as I did, that these pages are about him. They are not.)

To my friend, G.: His old LSAT books that he gave me, which I never opened. (I might have thrown these out, but it's the thought that counts.)

To my best friend, C.: My dogs and my passwords so she can delete our decades of digital nonsense. (As the constant in all things and the fundamental basis for life, she is largely absent from these volatile pages, but she is the ever-present, ever-fixed mark who keeps my brain intact.)

To halmoni (our father's mother): All of my jewelry and knickknacks, which she used to take from my room for "safekeeping" but really because they were sparkly and she wanted to put them on her shelf where she could look at them. (Nothing about what I am planning to do, please.)

To grandma (our mother's mother): All of my skincare products and the fancy dresses and coats she gave me. (Tell her I have gone to find grandpa.)

To grandpa (our mother's father): The Olympus camera that he gave me, the first camera I ever had. My language dictionaries. My record player, which he taught me how to fix and play. My records, most of which I took from him, anyway. (I started this before he left us. I suppose these revert to our parents now.)

To appa (our father): My books, except for the worn paperback copy of *Augustus*, in the hope that one day he might better understand who I was. My sincerest gratitude for his sacrifices for me and for our family, and my deepest regret and apology that I wasn't the child he wanted.

To umma (our mother): Everything else, including my grand piano (which is really her grand piano that I took) and *Augustus*, which she took from me years ago and never returned, so that maybe she will finally read past the prologue. My dearest, deepest love. I loved no one more than umma and I wish I could have been a prettier, kinder daughter, but I couldn't.

**I, being of unsounder mind, memory, and body,
create this Codicil, and declare the following amendments:**

To B.: The cutting board, chopsticks, and spoons he made me. They are heirloom pieces that deserve to be passed down to generations I will never create.

To Remember, I Write

In my mind, this memory is clear and unchanging. I have recorded it and written it and played it back and forth so many times that it has become fixed. I write it once more here, so that you might see more of me than the bedtime stories I tell you.

And also because some of this, as you will see, was a bit too awkward to say out loud to you, my little brother.

Anyway. In this memory, K. comes into the suite we shared in college and flops down on the single sofa, as he always does. He pushes up his glasses, which have silver wire frames. He is wearing a blue and black striped shirt. He has a magazine with him, something scientific, as usual. And he begins:

"Memory degrades every time you access it. People who tell you to keep memories alive by thinking about them often—they don't know what they're talking about."

Silence.

Then:

"Is that true?"

"Oh yeah, definitely. Each time you access a memory, you change something. Memory is not perfect. Vision isn't even perfect. It fools us the most, yet we rely on it the most. Isn't that strange? I remember my grandfather's house from my childhood in Albania. I think the walls are a dark orange. Each time I think about it, the color probably changes a little until the room is completely different from what it actually looks like. I'm sure if I went back now, it would be a totally different shade from what I remember."

Silence.

Then:

"So every time I think about this one memory, I'm losing it."

"Yeah. The best way to preserve a memory is to not think about it at all. Isn't that strange?"

Silence.

"Because, I mean, if we remembered everything—we can't. There is a reason memory isn't perfect. The brain automatically weeds out redundant information. Imagine having to sort through everything you have ever seen or learned or experienced. It would take forever to get what you needed."

Three Nights

Sometimes, in the moments before sleep, I am seized by a terror so acute that I feel it physically tear into my heart, crush my lungs. The first time it happened, I was six years old, and you were three. Umma and appa had told us to clean up the toy room, and while we were putting all the toys back, I found a book with a picture of an angel on it. *Embracing the Light*. It turned out to be a book on near-death experiences and the afterlife. I started reading it, and the next thing I knew, I looked up and you had meticulously put everything away while I sat there, oblivious, lost in the book and in my own head.

I made up an excuse for sleeping in our parents' room that night. I crept in with them and told them I had a stomachache. And again. And again. After the third night, appa took me to the pediatrician.

"Psychological, perhaps," the doctor said quietly, as if I would not hear. Our parents locked their door after that.

Brodmann Area (BA) 44/45 (Broca's Area)

In the memory of another conversation, I am messaging K. before the start of a new school year. And he asks me:

"Have I shown you my apartment?"

"Not yet."

"I don't really know how to describe it. There's this light coming in from the kitchen, and everything is sort of dark and almost fuzzy. Dreamlike, I guess."

"Softglow?"

"Yes. I have to say, I love your ability to give a name to things that I have been struggling to name. I spent three years saying 'There is something about the saffron yellow of street lamps.' Three years! And then you came along and said 'Yes, it is sickly.' And you hit it right on the money."

As I think back on this conversation, I am in a dark room, illuminated only by the yellow-orange haze of a street lamp filtering in through a smudged and dusty window that hasn't been cleaned since the house was built. He is lying back on a navy corduroy futon with his hands on his stomach.

None of this is true, of course, since I am not there in the apartment with him. I am miles away in a sun-filled room in Korea, in your room, using your computer while you're out playing squash with your friends. I am imagining a sickly softglow on a calm, moody night. A silicone chip somewhere remembers the conversation for me, word for word, while my brain fills in the details: imagination as memory.

Quincunx

Not all of my memories are deep and informative. Sometimes, they are stupid. Like K. saying:

"You know, I think if you take every irrational feeling in the universe and put them together, you get a woman."

Soon afterward, I realize that K. got this weak attempt at a witticism from a novel he recently read, and which he gives me to read. But even knowing this was idiocy didn't stop me from giving into my acute self-awareness and pathological need to be reasonable, to be not crazy.

I, the namer of things, took years to name what happened to me.

I looked outward, time and time again, to know that I was okay. To confirm that no one thought I was crazy, or delusional, or a liar. For so long, I revisited every detail in my head to evaluate whether my reaction was warranted, or if I should stop being so emotional.

I wonder later if this is how umma lived her life, never able to truly explain herself to the people she loved most.

"Why can't you leave me alone?" Halmoni might accuse.

"Why is my mother unhappy?" Appa might bark.

"Why is everyone so mad?" I might ask.

"I'm hungry," you might say, oblivious.

"Why do I put up with this?" Umma would mutter, silently, but still somehow loudly enough for just me to hear.

I hated what I thought was her passive-aggressive irrationality, but now I think it was the only way she could keep herself sane, with this one, tiny prick of resistance—invisible except for the fact that I was there to observe it, and she knew it.

It was a lesson, not a punishment.

I thought halmoni, who built this family on her back, was our bedrock. But in the end she, like all of us, clustered around umma. We lose one electron, then another, but our mother somehow, improbably, remains constant, steady, unfractured.

Six Sentences

Why am I spending these precious pages writing to you about K.? Because some of the things he says keep getting stuck in my head. Other memories are less about him, and more about how I am thinking in a particular moment. I hope—futilely, perhaps—that some truth about me emerges from these haphazard threads.

At this moment, for example, I am thinking about how to turn a life into a blurb. And I remember telling K.:

"I wrote your biography today."

I am in K.'s apartment, in the living room. We are eating burritos, and I am making a mess on purpose so I have an excuse not to look at his face.

"You wrote my biography?"

"We had this prompt in my writing seminar to write a life in six sentences, so I picked you."

"Really? Can I read it?"

"Sure. You're going to laugh, though." I hand him a sheet of paper and pretend to pay attention to a piece of shredded lettuce.

"What does this word say?"

"Oh, never mind. I'll just read it to you. My handwriting is indecipherable."

"Okay. I'm ready."

"Ten years in Albania, and then Istanbul. The Grand Bazaar, the alleyways, the chaos—his head never meets eye-level, he's so busy taking in the colorful madness. Ten years in Florida, where his high school is caged by barbed wire fences, and then New York City. His neck aches from the height of the buildings and his ears ring from the sound of the streets—one hundred lifetimes would not be enough to meet all of the people just on this stretch of island, and hear their stories. Words are not enough to capture this life—how freeing it would be to have pure channels of information." (He smiles softly at this phrase of his.) "Five years of engineering, and then neuroscience—he will find his answer here, in the brain, the last frontier."

He is silent.

"I used a lot of em dashes to get around the six sentences rule."

He is smiling faintly, far away. "I'm very flattered. Thank you."

Who cares about your Albanian friend, you might ask? What about us?

You are too shiny to distill into only six sentences, my silly brother. As for me, here in these pages is what I think of as my life. See if you can write six sentences to remember me by when I'm gone.

子. 홍옥선, maiden name 장

Enough about me for a moment. Here is some family history I expect you missed, being both the youngest and a boy.

Halmoni was born on January 5, 1925, in what we now call North Korea, or maybe it was on January 23, depending on which calendar you are using and how you calculate it. Cusp of the Rat and the Ox in the Chinese zodiac. She had five siblings: two older brothers, two younger brothers, and one younger sister.

The women in her village doted on her. One woman she knew when she was fourteen or fifteen years old had a kind heart but a strange temperament. When this woman was angry with her younger daughter, she would call her names and make fun of her eye. The daughter's left eye had been damaged somehow and had turned black. The daughter would fly into a rage and attack her mother, who, with her anger successfully displaced, would laugh and continue to taunt her daughter until the rage turned to tears and, eventually, sleep.

Halmoni was appalled that a woman would act this way to a child, but she maintains that the mother was a good woman. The woman's husband worked all through the night as a rickshaw driver and made enough money for his family to be comfortable. But the woman, who had no problem spending the money, never cleaned. Her house was a hovel, full of unwashed dishes with bits of rice and dirt. Halmoni felt sorry for the woman's husband, who worked so hard and came home to a mess. Halmoni has made a habit of cleaning dishes immediately after eating because she always says in her head that she will never be like that messy woman.

There was another woman, a childless woman whose husband was an alcoholic and who came home drunk and angry every night, partly because he couldn't have children. The woman invited halmoni over for lunch one day (the women in the neighborhood often invited halmoni in for a chat as they were lonely during the day) and served her heaps of food. The woman then said to her: "A woman, once married, may get very lonely and bored when her husband is away. She might want to skip proper meals out of unwillingness to take the trouble to cook for herself, but she must force herself to eat properly, to set the table properly. My mother told me this and I have wanted to tell all of the young women I can."

I didn't get it then. It makes sense to me now, when the act of walking to the refrigerator is an impossible quest and it feels like it would be easier to lie down and die.

Maybe this woman was trying to warn halmoni not to let devastating depression and the patriarchal prison of marriage bind her life.

Or maybe she was just telling halmoni how to be a dignified woman, and I should stop ascribing my modern feelings to an offhand remark.

Halmoni says she often thinks of them now, the women she knew in the village, the nice ones, the sweet ones, the funny ones, the spiteful ones. She was born in the north. She lived through Korean and Japanese atrocities. People lined up against the walls and shot in the streets, families torn apart. Or so she says. I'm not sure if that part is real, or if it's the dementia. But I think it is real. One of her younger brothers was taken prisoner and sent to a concentration camp in Siberia. He came out again many years later with one leg destroyed.

Halmoni married young, when her youngest brother was only five years old. She doted on him, buying him clothes and food. He was the youngest child and didn't listen to anyone else, but he was scared of her and listened to her.

On the eve of her wedding, he cried and begged her to stay, saying, "Sister, sister, I promise to be good, please don't get married."

Halmoni told him, "I'll be very close by, don't worry."

She fled to Seoul with her husband as soon as her first daughter was born.

BA 8. Blind Spot

K. and I have our weirder conversations out on his balcony or walking around campus. He's usually smoking a cigarette, which I would never do and you absolutely shouldn't do either.

"99.9 percent of what we see is interpolation by the brain. The actual signals, the stimuli in the outside world that we receive, they're such a small percentage of what's happening. The brain fills in the gaps for you, makes the connections. For example, you know you have a blind spot in your eye, right? Not like while you're driving, but when you are using your eyes every day."

"I read an article about that once. Or I probably just read the headline, I wasn't really paying attention."

K. flicks his cigarette and rests it on the balcony railing. "Here, stick out your left thumb and close your left eye. Now keep your right eye on your left thumb, and raise your right hand so the index finger is pointing at your thumb. Keep your hand at the level of your eyes. Remember, keep your eye on your thumb, not your index finger. Slowly bring your index finger closer to your thumb. At your blind spot, the tip of your finger will disappear. Well, I don't know if you'll be able to see here. It's pretty dark."

"Are you trying to make me look silly? I feel stupid."

"No, no, I'm serious. Try it."

"All right. I'm ready. So I hold out my thumb and watch only my thumb . . ."

"Right. No, don't move your finger so fast, do it slowly. Gradually. Keep your left eye closed. Keep going. Keep going."

"I see it! It shimmers away. It's right . . . *there* for me."

"Yeah, maybe fifteen degrees to the right. But you don't see a black spot, do you?"

"No, it becomes transparent, like I'm seeing through it."

"Exactly. That's your brain, filling in the gaps. It's interpolating information from the environment, but it's not what you really see. Even blinking."

"What about blinking?"

"You don't notice it most of the time. It's not as if you consciously see a black interruption in your vision. Your brain makes these decisions for you, and you don't know it. I don't think you decide anything. Like in that study with monkeys, where the researchers could predict what the monkey was going to do before the monkey did anything, just by where the parts of the brain lit up. Fuck, man. We're all just robots."

the man walked, with only his silver lyre, without food, without water, without sleep.

"That's impossible. And dumb."

He was really sad, okay? His new wife had just died.

"Orpheus, more like BORE-pheus. Maybe that's why Eurydice dies. Of boredom."

Just listen. He played and sang as he walked, and the marvel of his music was such that the wind stayed ever at his back. Fountains sprang up, eager to quench his thirst, and burbled back into the soil when he was sated. Birds flocked and trees bowed to offer him dates and berries and seeds as he passed.

On the tenth day, the man arrived at a sparkling bay with a green marble cave in the distance. He played his lyre once more, and the waves rose up to usher him gently into the yawning maw of the cave. Sunlight filtered in through cracks in the stone roof and illuminated the slick pathway, which glowed a vivid purple from a graveyard of spiny snails that flanked either side.

And he plunged into his grief.

As he descended, shadows seeped into the cave and blotted out the sound of the sea and the light of the sky.

And he grew afraid. He plucked his lyre for comfort, and he felt a gentle breeze guide him down into the abyss. When he emerged from the marble cavern into a vast expanse of steel-gray crags, the darkness clung to him as a thick cloak, shielding him from the piercing eyes of the ferryman guarding the veil between the living and the dead.

> "What about the dog? I thought there was a dog there. Like Lilly, if she had three heads. Cereal Bus. Cervantes? Sir Butthead."

Cerberus. Usually pronounced with a K sound. The man—

> "Did he pet the dog?"

Though the man longed to pet the plush fur of each dog head, he dared not risk waking the fluffy creature from its deep sleep. Shrouded in shadow, he crept past its three heads until its snores were far behind him. And then he began to play his lyre again, at first slowly and then ever more quickly, in time with the beating of his heart.

> "What's the point of hiding yourself in a cloak of darkness if you announce yourself to the whole underworld by saying, 'Anyway, here's Wonderwall'?"

His song was so beautiful that no one thought to stop him. As he walked, he passed unforgettable sights—a crowned figure pushing a boulder up an unending hill, a naked body spinning on a wheel of flame, a parched skeleton reaching for water that became dust in his hands. For a moment, the man's song stayed the sliding boulder, suspended the twirling circle of fire, slowed the flow of water. But he went on, and so did they.

Throughout the sunless domain, the man watched shades drinking from a winding smoky river and coming away with empty faces. Only those who drank from a shimmering golden pool were permitted to pass into a glen of light. Though he longed to explore these mysteries, he walked on, into the heart of the dark kingdom, where two obsidian thrones loomed in a courtyard of pomegranate trees.

It was here that he would move the Queen of the Icy Heart and the God of the Undergloom with his pleading lament. For the Unseen One must know what it was to be separated from his love, and the Queen must know what it was to be taken away from her life. The shades and the rivers and the trees and the rocks would echo with his love for his wife. He would grasp her hand and lead her out of perdition, from this sunless kingdom back into a brilliant, joyful life of music and dancing and light. And they would be happy again. For he was only one side of a blade of grass, and she was the other—indivisible.

"What if you peel the grass apart? I do that all the time."

Two sides of a piece of paper, then. Put that down, you're going to give yourself a papercut.

BA 10.
I remember . . .

Halmoni was hit by a motorbike once. I must have been three or four, because it happened while we were still living in 이태원 in Korea. You weren't born yet. I remember her walking over the hill that led down from our apartment. It was a dazzling, clear day, one of those rare days that the sky was pure blue and the sun shone yellow. She walked up the curve to the left, her leather loafers slapping against the pavement and her curly black hair waving in the breeze. She was smiling and humming to herself. Even though the hill wasn't that steep, it was such that you could look forward into the horizon and it seemed as if you were walking into shimmering air.

A motorbike came zooming up out of nowhere. It never slowed down, just hit her straight on. It was a black motorbike, probably out to deliver a package. And there she was, halmoni, her head split open on the pavement.

Except I saw none of this. I wasn't there. I don't remember where I was. Maybe at preschool, maybe in my room playing with toys, maybe down at the corner store begging umma to buy me grape candy. What I know is this: I wasn't with halmoni when her head hit the ground.

But these images are here in my head, clear as that day. The memory is fabricated through retellings and revisionings and reconstructions, but it is true. Its contents are true. Its existence in my head is false.

She was rushed to the hospital. Somehow, she didn't die. Surgery repaired her skull. The hospital room was small and the rooms were yellow.

Umma and appa brought me in to see her when she woke up and was recovered enough to receive visitors.

This memory is real, I think. Her head looked smaller to me, shrunken, slanted, as if the left side of her skull had been lopped off. I asked her if that's what they had done and she laughed and said, yes, yes they took part of my head, here it is, don't you see? And she pointed to a gray rock on a shelf near her bed. I really thought that rock was her skull. Her head looked that way partly because the doctors had cropped her hair close to the skull, so they could operate. But for years, I was convinced they had taken part of her head in that surgery.

"I thought you were supposed to be the smart one in our family."

I learned later that they did take out part of her head, temporarily. They had to do a decompressive craniectomy to relieve the pressure in her brain from the trauma.

"Calm down, doctor."

They took one of her skull plates and sewed it into her stomach for safe-keeping before they could put it back into her head.

"They WHAT?"

It's true. And then they sewed it back into her head once she was stable. I remember being curious as she recovered, and then excited that she was coming home, and then the accident becoming part of our family lore.

Umma remembers this differently. She remembers the Furies descending upon the hospital and side-eyeing her, primed to hound her to the grave if halmoni didn't pull through.

"Hound, because Furies have dog heads. I get it. I'm a genius. But why were people mad at umma? It wasn't her fault."

No, but umma was the one who took care of halmoni, even though halmoni was appa's mother, not hers. Umma might not have been bound to halmoni by blood, but her role as appa's wife was enough to place the burden of halmoni's life on her.

I, of course, was oblivious, occupied with wondering whether it hurt to be missing part of your skull, and did this mean half of your head was squishy and light, and if so, whether that meant your head would always be drooping to one side.

I didn't notice how halmoni changed after that, how even after she left the hospital and her hair grew back, she never shook off the shadow of death.

Halmoni refers to the accident often, at least to me. She made a full, almost miraculous, recovery, but whenever she forgets something or gets confused, she mentions the motorbike. Still, decades of Korean automotive engineering and steel couldn't take her head away. The soft flesh of her mind won out, in the end.

November 17

What was it?

A memory so far away now that it feels like a fairy tale. (The kind you tell as a warning.) A memory I have accessed so many times that it has degraded, K. might say, if he knew.

I didn't know. I was confused. I looked out of the window and saw one of those bright mornings that hurts your eyes and fools you into thinking it's later than it really is. The clock blinked 6:38 in dark red letters. I sat up. I didn't know where my shirt was. I didn't know where I was.

"Good morning."

What was it?

I woke up to find my body no longer my own. I found my shirt and I left to the sound of a cheerful goodbye. Did this person know what he had done?

I called C. in a daze. You remember her, she drove me to visit you up at Andover that time we brought you eleven boxes of samosas. I told her I had woken up without my shirt, but I said it as if I had intended for this to happen. She laughed and asked me for details, and I told her I would talk to her later.

This is one of those awkward things it's easier for me to relay in writing.

I went to the university health center to see a nurse. I tried to find the words to name the night.

—Were you drinking?

Yes? Is that relevant?

—Go home and sleep it off. You'll feel better in the morning.

Don't I need an exam?

—I don't think so. You just need some sleep.

I went home and didn't sleep.

Months later, I saw him, somewhere, with another girl whose skin and

41

eyes and hair looked like mine. He smirked at me and said, unprompted, "You know how vain I am." I didn't know what this meant, but his tone turned my blood to ice.

I am sorry, other girl.

I don't remember much of that year. I remember I ate, and ate, and ate, and appa, upon seeing me, summoned me home to Korea and forced me to take a break from school so I could lose weight. I was humiliated and furious and secretly grateful to have an excuse to hide myself away.

I don't remember what I told you about why I left school, but you didn't ask me any questions, which relieved me. I hoped to one day tell you the whole story, as much a lesson for you as a cautionary tale about me.

Home was a strange word for Korea then, as it is now. Each time I am home, I am a stranger in my own country. The country of our mother, our father, our grandmothers. The country of my skin and my eyes and my hair. The country of our language. It is a parallel world, almost the same but with something gone awry. I am uneasy here, among these people who look like each other and like me. Unlike me, you always fit in so well here—anywhere, really—even though my Korean was better than yours. (Grammatically, anyway. You had a particular gift for direct translation, like that time you wanted to call me a butthead but umma and appa had put in a new rule that we had to speak Korean for the whole day, and you came up with 엉덩이 머리.)

The sky here is different. A yellowish green haze covers the sun. Light is prisoner to these dusty, swarming particles, as I am a prisoner to this language.

I could walk unnoticed. A dot in a line, indistinguishable. Instead, when I see a foreigner, I ask what time it is, to prove I speak their language, too.

she and her sister and her younger brothers slept in the same bed, under a window that stayed cool in the shadow of the mountain that guarded them.

And then she became a woman.

> "If this is about Eurydice's changing body,
> we already did that in middle school."

Did they show you the video where the parents draw a uterus with pancake batter? And then they all eat the pancake?

> "What? No, we had a demonstration with a
> banana. What unhinged class did you take?"

I guess they only did the pancake video for the girls. Anyway.

As a gift into womanhood, and to prepare her for when she would leave for marriage, her father built her a small room all to herself, next to the one her older brothers shared. In the mornings, her father and older brothers went out to hunt and to check the trees around them for danger of fire. She and her mother worked the loom, and when there was no more wool to spin or weave, she sat in the meadow behind their cottage and watched her younger sister and brothers pet the dogs and call to the birds. They ran through grass that grew tall with wildflowers and cattails that tickled their knees. By the pond at the edge of the meadow, they admired the turtles and fed the fish.

In the afternoons, when it grew hot and the younger ones napped inside, she stole away, up the forested mountain, to a stream that flowed through a clearing in the trees. There, in the crystal waters, she bathed and luxuriated in her solitude.

In the evenings, when her father and older brothers returned, they ate together and told stories around the hearth. Her father told her of this man or that man's glorious exploits and generous offers of gifts in return for her hand in marriage. She laughed each one off as too tall or too pale or too old or too young, spinning yarns around each of their imagined defects. Her japes masked her worry that one night, her father might run out of patience and decide for her. But he only shook his head, sighing, and laughed with her. And, pushing away her fear that one day she would be taken from her home, she sighed with relief under the illusion that she could remain with her family forever.

One afternoon at the mountain stream, as she dried her skin in the sunlight and draped herself in her cotton tunic, she heard in the distance the faint ringing of a lyre and a clear voice of rich honey that stilled her heart and filled her with warmth.

She hid behind two intertwined trees and waited for the voice to grow closer. A man with a silver lyre appeared in the clearing. His shoulders were broad and sun-kissed, shining like a field of golden wheat. His straw-colored hair and beard were neatly trimmed. His left arm, bare and muscled, held the lyre that he plucked with his right hand. His fingers were thick and calloused, more the fingers of a soldier than of a musician. But they plucked the taut strings with unmatched grace.

She waited to see if anyone followed behind—a band of rowdy brothers, perhaps, or a nymph-like wife—but he moved alone, and she found that she felt no fear.

She stepped out from behind the trees. Startled, the man stepped back, and a silence fell over the clearing.

And she asked him: "Will you play another song? I didn't mean to surprise you. I only wanted to get a closer look at your . . . lyre."

"What a liar."

The man smiled and began to play once more. As she moved closer to him, she saw that his hair and beard glinted with copper in the light. His eyes were a greenish-gray, also flecked with copper. She circled him as he played, entranced by the music.

And then he stopped. "I was on my way to visit a friend, and I'm afraid I'm already late. But if you wish, I will pass through here tomorrow, before I return home to my kingdom."

She studied his face, as if to ponder her answer, though they both knew that she would return. He bowed to her with a smile and sang his way past her. She remained in the clearing until the echoes of his voice faded into the wind.

He was waiting for her the next day when she arrived at the mountaintop. She sat down on the rock next to the stream, and he sang to her about a quest for a fleece of shining gold.

"Like, *the* golden fleece? From the Argonaut story?"

The very one. Remember, there were fifty Argonauts, and Orpheus was one of them.

He regaled her also with stories and details that didn't make it into his songs, and her eyes alternately widened in wonder and narrowed in disbelief.

And she said to him: "We don't have golden sheep here. But not as much murder, either. So I think I prefer my mountain to your ship."

The man laughed and tugged lightly on a strand of her hair.

"Is it your mountain, lady?" he asked.

And she replied: "I rarely see other people here. We live at the base of the mountain, and my father and brothers hunt here often. The mountain has been kind to us. We don't live for glory, but for each other."

She stood then. "Which reminds me, I have to go back home now. Thank you for the songs."

His fingers closed around her right wrist, and she wondered if she should be afraid. But his touch was gentle, and he came no closer.

"Will you return tomorrow?"

"Don't you need to get back home?"

He shrugged. "I have no shortage of guest-friends here, and I am in no rush to leave."

Did she blush then?

> "Ooh. Orpheus and Eurydice sitting in a tree. Eff-you-sea-kay-eye-en-gee."

Are you going to behave?

> "WAIT. Isn't she like twelve years old?"

A bit older, fourteen or fifteen. Maybe sixteen.

> "How old is Orpheus?"

Older. Definitely an adult. Blame the ancients.

"Gross. And then what happened?"

She slipped away to the stream every afternoon thereafter, not only to enjoy the cool waters but to listen to the man with the lyre. Her sister and her younger brothers begged her to take them, but she sang them to sleep before leaving, in case they tried to follow her. The cloth she wove in the mornings grew elaborate, telling new stories of dragons and potions and sea voyages.

One evening, when she returned home, her father and older brothers were already there, conversing with a strange man in the meadow behind their cottage. The man was tall, with golden eyes and a strange curve in his lips that formed a smile but suggested something else. Bees crowned his dark hair.

She stepped into the cottage unnoticed and clasped her hands. "Mother, please."

Her mother shook her head. "He is wealthy and powerful and beloved of the gods. With only a glance of his eyes, he controls smoke and fire. It is time. Your father has been very patient with you."

"I don't like him."

"You haven't even met him. And you liking him isn't required."

"What if I were already promised to someone else? Someone just as wealthy and powerful and beloved of the gods."

Her mother gave her a sharp look. "What do you mean, promised? Do you mean the man with the lyre who has been singing you the stories you have been weaving each morning? As if your sister and brothers wouldn't tell me? As if I wouldn't notice?"

She did not avoid her mother's gaze. "Just. What if?"

Her mother handed her a bowl of olives and bread. "If, if, if. It is for your father to judge, my darling girl. Only he can choose." And her mother nudged her to the table at the hearth.

The golden-eyed man barely glanced at her during dinner, except to say that she would need to begin wearing a veil once he took her to his home. She remained silent, relieved and annoyed that no response was required of her. She did not say a word until he was gone and her father turned to her. She fell to the ground and threw her arms around his knees in supplication.

"Father, please. Please, not him."

Her father lifted her up with both arms—not gently, but not roughly, either. "It is time. And he has much to offer our family. Almost as much as he has power to destroy us. I have accepted his offer."

"Undo it. Find any excuse. For I have promised myself to another."

Her father laughed. "Promised or given? No matter. It is not for you to choose the man who will take you. This man is wealthy and power-ful and beloved of the gods. With only a glance of his eyes, he controls smoke and fire. Can you say the same of your imaginary friend?"

"He is not imaginary. He comes from a wealthy and powerful kingdom, where he will rule after his father has gone to the wide-gated house be-low. And he shall not take me before I am ready."

Her father stopped laughing. "Is this a dream? A tale? A trick?"

And she replied: "I will marry him here tomorrow, if you wish. Only, send a message to the golden-eyed man this night that you decline his offer. Father, please. At least let it be someone I know."

Her father was silent a long while.

And then: "I am trusting you, girl, that this man you say you have promised yourself to is as worthy as the guest we had tonight. Swear on our mountain, and I will send your brother this night to decline."

"I swear it." She bowed her head.

"Then it shall be so."

In the morning, she cut her finished piece from the loom. As the sun grew high, she ran up to swim in the stream and calm her jumping heart. As she waited for the man with the lyre, she saw far below her a wisp of smoke rising from some hearth, bringing to her the scent of charred and roasted flesh. And she wondered what it was like to be a god receiving holy sacrifices. Closing her eyes, she breathed in, listening to the burble of the stream and the rustle of leaves, and she drifted into a dream.

She awoke, smiling, to the man with the lyre calling out to her. She jumped up and draped over his shoulder the cloak she had woven.

"You have brought my songs to life."

She nodded, a flush rising in her cheeks, and spoke carefully. "Will you teach me to play the lyre? I wish to learn from you, even if it takes all of our days."

He looked up at her. "The lyre does indeed take a long time to learn. A lifespan, some say. Will we have a lifespan together?"

She studied his face and masked any sign of triumph. He was studying her with a small, anxious smile, which she reflected in her own face.

"We will. If you promise not to take me away from here before I am ready. And if you agree we may return to the house of my mother and my father whenever I wish."

"Did she just trick him into proposing to her?"

49

It was either that or the bees. He took her hands and touched his forehead to hers. "I swear it on this stream. I will follow you to your cottage this evening bearing gifts."

"My father and mother will be glad to receive you. But now, while we are alone—" She began to gather leaves and flowers and, after a moment, he did the same. He placed a wreath of wildflowers on her head, and she on his.

"Are they going to Coachella?"

They're eloping. And, with a kiss, they parted, he to gather gifts and she to ready dinner.

She ran down the mountain, shy and giddy, bursting to tell her mother and her sisters and her brothers and her father to prepare for the man who would be coming to their cottage.

But the cottage was no more.

There was only ash and ember and bone. She stopped still, choking on the acrid smoke. It was then that she realized the smoke she had inhaled on the mountaintop had come from the burning bodies of her family. And in the distance, she saw through the haze the golden-eyed man stalking toward her with a dark smile on his face.

"Why is he so creepy!"

She ran. In her shock and anguish, she did not feel the sharp bite at her ankle, and did not live to see the viper slithering away from the fire.

She saw only darkness.

When the darkness lifted, she found herself stepping off of a boat into a meadow of asphodel.

"Is she dead?"

Extremely.

"So the bee guy set them all on fire? All because she rejected him?"

One might be led to suspect such a thing. Don't be like His Creepiness of the Bees.

Shrouded in the pallid undergloom, she wandered through the meadow until she came to a cypress tree. Climbing its sturdy branches, she peered around from the top, from where she could see a vast, sunless domain. In the distance, she saw a shining golden pool guarded by dark forms, and beyond that, a glen filled with light. Through the asphodel flowed a smoky river, its banks thick with drinking shades.

"She shouldn't drink from the river. She'll forget everything."

So you were paying attention! She avoided both the river and the pool, and instead wandered through the endless meadows. She studied the face of every shade she passed—or tried, anyway. Some still had the sharp features of the recently living, and they nodded at her. Others, translucent and faded, smiled blankly in her general direction. Still others did not greet her at all, for they no longer had faces. They were forms that barely remembered to be forms, wisps of air reflecting the pale gray gloom.

And she wondered if she would ever find them, or they would ever find her—her mother, her sister, her brothers, her father. They had been swept below just before she had arrived, and she had been so sure they would be there to welcome her. She wondered if they were angry with her for not having been with them, for having spent her afternoons away on the mountaintop listening to the man with the lyre, for having ignited the flames with her rejection of the man with the golden eyes.

51

"But it wasn't her fault. And she *wanted* to stay with her family."

That's not how guilt works. Or blame.

Though she searched and searched, she found no one, and no one found her. Instead, she found herself by the smoky river again and again, pondering its obscure depths. She must have wandered a thousand lifespans by now, and greeted every shade in asphodel, but she was still alone. She had never feared death, and indeed, had thought it a gift when she had collapsed onto the burning bones of her family, out of that strange man's grasp. But she had not realized that she would endure the eternity of death alone.

"But I thought she only just died."

Time is different in the underworld. Or maybe there is no time.

And then she heard in the distance the faint plucking of a lyre and a voice of rich honey, and the sound created in her mind a muted echo, a shade of a remembrance, and she struggled to grasp at the form dancing at the edges of her memory. She sank to her knees once more in the asphodel.

A burst of color arced before her eyes and a rainbow spoke with the Queen's icy voice. "Your husband has come to take you back with him."

She wavered, but did not reply.

"Don't you miss the warmth of the sun? You chose your husband freely, did you not?"

She paused. "I chose him more than I did not choose him."
The rainbow danced above her. "Then why do you not rejoice?"

"I am looking for my mother and my sister and my brothers and my father."

The rainbow fell silent. When it spoke again, the Queen's voice was softer. "The golden pool can show you the way to your family. But if you drink from it, you will be bound to this world without end."

She did not reply, and the rainbow went on. "If you drink from the smoky river, enough to dissolve your memory of this place, you may return with your husband. But you may never find your family again. For while you live the remainder of your life above, your family may drink enough of the smoky river to be reborn into new bodies, with no memory of you."

"Do souls get reincarnated?"

In some versions, they do. If they drink from the River Lethe and wash away their past, they can cross back over into a new life.

The rainbow faded away with an echo of the Queen's voice: "You may approach the throne to look upon your husband. And then you must choose."

She looked into the smoky river and to the golden pool in the distance.

"And then? What did she pick?"

Bedtime now.

13 조선Ships

Halmoni speaks to me sometimes still. I try to grasp all the words.

Her time under Japanese and then communist rule instilled in her fear and resentment. With the departure of the Empire of Japan came a proxy war and, eventually, Eternal Leader Kim Il-Sung.

None of the rest of halmoni's family would defect to Seoul because the government had their uncle, and if they saw a deserter in the family, they would hurt or kill him. But when halmoni got married, she was classified as her husband's family, so she was able to flee. She left behind a garden of flowers and animals—dogs, cats, birds, turtles, fish.

Her husband died young, in his early fifties, of a heart attack in a park. He refused for years to take his blood pressure medication, which destroyed his heart and tore appa's in two. He might have been a pilot, but I don't know. I never asked.

Halmoni brought her three children to New York with the equivalent of twenty-five dollars, or so appa used to tell us. They all worked through school, including appa even though he was only a kid, and they paid rent on an apartment in Queens for two years until they could afford to buy a house. Halmoni worked at a sewing factory because she knew no English and couldn't do anything else. She had a hard time learning the sewing. Sometimes, her manager would be difficult and tell her to redo everything, so she would stay through the night to redo it. She became more experienced and later mentored the women who came over from Korea to start a new life. When the company began to upgrade its sewing machines, she bought the old one and kept it for thirty years.

When she is upset (that isn't quite the right word for it—the right word is 속상해), she goes to her sewing machine and hems anything. At first, she was afraid of the loud noise, but now the sewing machine is a dear friend. When something goes wrong, she knows exactly what to do. I asked her to teach me to sew and she says I won't ever need to know such a thing.

When we were growing up in New Jersey, she made playclothes for us that we wore to rags outside. Comfy shirts and elastic shorts made of purple cotton with a pattern of yellow pansies. She had a small annex to her room where she created garments for us and for herself. On the walls, she displayed curios she gathered on her walks, magpie that she was, and sang hymns to us as we sat safe and snug under her sewing table.

When I was older, and you were away at school, halmoni still sewed me clothes, but I didn't think they were my style and I left them untouched. She lost her temper with me one night and screamed at me about how ungrateful I was, and how she was going to tell umma and appa about the secret snacks I had stashed away in my room. Of all the things I remember, now that she has lost her past and her voice and most of her brain, what I remember most is deep and abiding shame: me, an ungrateful brat, showing no regard for her life's work and her love for me.

14 Enigma Variations

K. told me once:

"Emergence is one of the most beautiful concepts in the universe. Do you know what emergence is?"

"I can guess from the name."

"Say you have two basic properties. Or just two simple things. Like this song playing in this video. The song itself is nice, but nothing special. The images that play are ordinary. But you put them together and they combine to make something totally different and new."

"Emergence."

"Emergence."

"That the sum is more than its parts."

"Right. It's an elegant concept. I think so, anyway."

Soft piano playing over a reel of snow. Exit music for a film.

'15. Leaving Elba

Was I in exile?

I resented every moment I had to be away. With appa, pushing me about my weight and insisting that I stop scribbling stories and instead apply my writing to something useful, like law school. With umma, withholding food and trying to get me to explain what could possibly be making me so sad. With halmoni, telling me that she would die soon. With myself, trying to forget.

I treasured every moment I had away. With appa, climbing up a temple in Tibet and shielding our eyes from the blaze of a holy lake. With umma, walking along the Han River and going to museums that she pretended to love, for me. With halmoni, spinning yarns about her childhood and mine.

With myself, traveling to places I had only read about. I jumped through springy bogs and hiked through fields of golden-purple heather, silver karst, deep emerald moss.

Did I come back healed?

Enough to not look back. Enough that when I moved into a beautiful, old house and met beautiful, new people, it wasn't the first thing I spilled when I introduced myself. Enough that by the time K. explained glutamate receptors to me, I had moved on to another trauma entirely.

For 16 Hours Each Day . . .

halmoni used to follow a regular schedule. She would get up at five in the morning to eat breakfast on account of the medication she had to take. She prayed to God every morning, every meal, every night, every day. She still says to me:

"What have I to be afraid of? God has always helped me, guided me, protected me, made my life rich, and he always will. I've nothing to fear."

After breakfast, she watched television or cleaned. Her favorite part of day was when you went off to school and appa left for work, with both of you saying, "안녕히 다녀오겠습니다" in the morning and "다녀왔습니다" at night.

"Speak English; this is America."

We're literally in Seoul. And the words sound stilted in English: "I will come back well" and "I have returned."

"You're right; that was weird."

If she had class at the senior center, she went early in the morning to exercise, and then to English or computer class. Now, I think about all the times she asked me to teach her English and how to use email. I think about how begrudgingly I taught her, and how patiently you took up the task.

"I didn't really teach her that much. And you taught her a lot, too. You taught me how to teach her."

Maybe. I don't know. If she liked the menu for lunch at the senior center, she paid two dollars for a lunch ticket. She and her friends chatted in their free time and bought each other coffee, sometimes up to five cups. Then they went around to the park or the bus or the marketplace.

If she didn't like the lunch menu, she came home for lunch and tended to her gardening or watched television or worked on her sewing. Then you would come home, Part A of Part Two of her favorite part of the day. She would make you dinner, and afterward listen to Bible study on tape or radio, and pray. At eight o'clock, she watched her favorite drama and went to sleep at nine.

She built a family around herself because she as good as lost hers, but she was still alone. At least when we lived in New Jersey, she could be close to her daughters, and to me when I was younger, before I became a selfish monster who didn't have time to take walks with her or keep her company when she sewed. Here in Korea, she has friends but no one else to talk with all day.

Line 17. Under The Harvest Moon

Sometimes, K. and I head to the park. Not the one with the baseball diamond where we took Lilly that time you visited, but the one along the heights overlooking the city.

Darkness, sickly yellow streetlights, clandestine couples on benches and behind trees. And he might say something like:

"Before I die, all I want to do is live out certain images I have in my head. I want to race down a desert highway in a Coupe de Ville convertible, cops after me, sun setting, my Bonnie with a shotgun in the passenger seat. And the right music playing in the background."

"You would die."

"Probably. But at least I would have lived it. The point is, I want to live out these images."

Of course he does.

"In fact, say sometime in the future, they find the capability to simulate anything you want in the brain. You've seen *The Matrix*, right? The first one."

"There's only one."

He laughs. "Only one, right. Say they suppress the part of your brain that controls movement"—he touches the back of his neck, and so do I—"so that you don't injure yourself. The way your brain suppresses movement in your sleep. Say they do that, and then they are able to feed images and emotions into your brain. Think about it. It would be so amazing. It would be a dark day for the world, but it would change everything."

"People would never want to do anything else. How could they?"

"They wouldn't have to. Everything would be in the brain."

"Would it be real? Not real?"

"What is real, anyway? Everything is in your brain already. Say they found the neural correlates for everything—love, for example. They find the thing in my brain that makes me fall in love. What is the difference between somebody else causing that, and something in my brain being switched on? Or even the correlates for a specific person. You could bring the dead back to life, if you knew enough about them. I mean, it would only be for yourself, but they would be there with you."

"It's not the same."

"Why not? Your brain is capable of anything." He waves his cigarette at me in a way I find irritating.

"Because interacting with other people isn't only neurons firing. You react to them. They're something new. If you're stuck in your head all the time, it's self-limiting. There is no outside."

"But you're like that now. Everything somebody else says, there is no way for you to understand exactly what they mean with their knowledge and thoughts and experiences. You have to adapt it to your own being to understand. What's the difference?"

I shake my head at him as he leans over the stone parapet looking down on the city lights. "You cannot create a whole other human being. You'll know it's not real. And you would be incredibly lonely."

"But we are! Everybody is lonely. Right now. Everybody. You think these distractions, other people, you think any of this cures that?"

"You're always approaching this as a neuroscientist. There is more to us than cells."

"That's the thing. People have this view that there's this homunculus in their brain pulling levers here and there, controlling everything. Your 'mind' or 'self' or whatever. Descartes and all of these philosophers, they had this idea of mind and matter being separate. But what if there's just—"

"Mind."

"No. Matter."

I laugh. "Oh."

"Your body. Your skin. You think of your skin as yours, but not as you. You think you are something else. Your mind, your self, whatever. Something you can't touch. But what is that? It's just your brain. Synapses in your head."

"But—"

"Of course, like you say, I have to hope for something more, or else it would be devastating. But that doesn't mean you can ignore this and not think about it because you're afraid. Once you examine all of the possibilities and still believe in something more, then maybe there's hope. Or maybe there's nothing. I don't know."

He keeps talking, but the rest of the conversation fades in my head, under the control of my homunculus or whatever, and all I am left with is the notion of:

What if you could bring someone back from the dead, even if only in your head? Would it be the same?

THE PARK IS NOW CLOSED.

We walk, and we are home.

$$1.8320128(17) \times 10^{-24} \text{ cal/}^\circ\text{R}.$$

"Do you know what entropy is?"

(A pop quiz for you, the only science-minded person in our family aside from grandpa.)

I remember K. helping me unpack, and I wonder if his question is a comment on the mess that is my room, but he looks thoughtful.

"The state of things to tend toward disorder. Or something."

"Not exactly. I mean, yes, that is true, that is what people think of when they think of entropy. But that's sort of simplistic. Yes, there is an increase of disorder. But it takes work to keep everything ordered. To live is to fight entropy. You, for example, are a higher-level being, an ordered collection of molecules and cellular functions. It takes a lot of energy to keep you as you are. So when you die, your cells spread out."

"Lovely."

"Yeah. Entropy returns nature to a more balanced state. Less work, more balance. The natural state of things is to be balanced, for cells to be spread equally. It's elegant. Creates a level playing field. It's one of my favorite concepts. That and emergence."

"I was going to say I prefer your concept of emergence."

"I also like emergence. Entropy and emergence. At least I've got those two things."

1-978. Andover Parents' Weekend

Thank you for registering for Parents' Weekend.

Please save this page as a record of your transaction.

Confirmation Number: PAA1506905-2235252

K. and G. drove me up to Andover once so we could pretend to be your parents and see how much trouble you were causing in high school.

Before we met up with you, I showed them around the campus designed by Olmsted, the seal designed by Paul Revere, the silver sculpture on the Great Lawn that is definitely a penis ringed by a bush, even though the school won't admit it.

We met you in English class, if you remember, where you were reading Faulkner. You made faces at me while the teacher wasn't looking.

G., meanwhile, was listening to every word, enraptured. "I cannot believe this is a high school. I didn't know what a thesis statement was until I got to college. How is your brother writing a paper about Faulkner?"

I introduced myself to your teacher after class and told him I was playing your mom for the day. He told me how much you had improved over the semester, that you're doing much better now with Faulkner than with Shakespeare, and that you're a delight to have in class.

"See? I'm a delight."

"More importantly, do I really have to sit through both physics and math now? Pretending to be your mom is the worst."

We sent K. and G. to explore the campus so they wouldn't have to sit through another two hours of class. The physics teacher told me what a pleasure it was to read your thorough, confident solutions, and your math teacher ran out of synonyms for "excellent" in explaining to me how you were by far the strongest student in the class and should take multivariable calculus and linear algebra the next semester, which confirmed for me that we hatched on opposite ends of the gene pool.

"I have no idea how we are related. How do you get a 102 percent in AP Calculus, but you can't read Hamlet properly?"

"Who cares if Hamlet wanted bees or not to have bees. I'm hungry."

K. and G. met us at a Thai restaurant downtown, where I ordered the noodles I had been dreaming about since I graduated, years earlier. You and K. got into some discussion about theoretical physics, and G. and I were laughing about how out of our depth we were.

I was signing the check when you stopped me.

"How did you do that?"

"What?"

"You didn't use a calculator for the tip."

"I always tip twenty percent."

"But how do you know what twenty percent is?"

I remember staring at you, thinking you were joking. "You're not serious."

"Tell me how!"

"You . . . move the decimal over and multiply by two."

". . . Oh."

"I'm telling your math teacher."

"Nooooooo, then she will know I am a fraudulent!"

"So will your English teacher if he hears that sentence."

We brought you back up to campus, and K. and G. went to go start the car.

And I asked you, "Do you need money?"

I don't even know why I asked, and I handed you some cash, which I am sure you used very responsibly. "Don't use this all at once. Don't use it on anything that will get you kicked out of school. And if you must get an ID, get a real ID from another Asian guy. He doesn't even have to be Korean, because no one can ever tell us apart."

Your sheepish smile told me you already had one, and I rolled my eyes. "Just don't be stupid." I gave you a hug.

What I didn't tell you then is what I remembered in that moment. I remembered you coming with umma to drop me off for my first year of college, and me being so angry at the time that appa had confiscated all of my cash and revoked my access to my bank account because he didn't think I could be responsible with my money. You handed me a bag of candy before you left, and I didn't know why you were blushing.

Only later when I settled into my dorm did I realize that you had stuffed a wad of tens and twenties—all the money you must have owned at the time, since you were fourteen and just starting at Andover— around a box of orange tic tacs, my favorite. I called you and cried, and you said it wasn't a big deal, that I needed it more than you did since umma could give you more money if you needed it (true), and, anyway, you were going to charge me humongous interest fees.

All I said instead before I got in the car to leave Andover was:

"Be good."

"I am! I'm good at everything."

"Except calculating tip."

"Don't tell anyone!"

Sorry, brother. I couldn't help it.

20. The Resistance

Our other grandma, our mother's mother, sewed clothes for high-end designers. A fashion house once sent her a coffee table book, a retrospective of their pieces, with an inscription and signature honoring her years of hard work. We flipped through the book and she told me how difficult it was to sew this intricate wedding dress (inexplicably shot in the middle of the ocean, rendering the dress unusable), because the buttons kept popping off.

She pointed to another woman and said she had heard that this woman was famous, and the woman had been extraordinarily graceful and easy to dress. And I laughed and told her:

"Grandma, that's Beyoncé."

Grandma, too, had a huge sewing machine in the house where umma grew up. A little house in Edison, New Jersey, with a wind-chime on the stained-glass front door that created rainbows in the afternoon on the carpeted stairs. An old grandfather clock kept the time, and we thought we might find Narnia in there. Our grandparents tended a vegetable garden in the yard at the side of the house and prided themselves on feeding us the peppers and pumpkins and tomatoes they grew for us. The last picture I have of grandpa is of you and him carrying bags of mulch out from the garage into the garden, and you wearing a giant straw hat with goofy sunglasses.

Grandma and grandpa never thought of themselves as rich, but scrimped enough to send umma to a liberal arts college and an Ivy League business school while appa worked nights to get his college degree and MBA from a city school. Maybe I shouldn't have remarked on that difference to you, because when it came time for college essays, you wrote:

"My father and his mother came to America with twenty-five dollars, and my dad worked hard enough to become a CEO. My mother, on the other hand, was kind of a slacker because her parents grew up rich."

Years after grandpa died, when you were in college, we—our mother's mother, our mother, and me—took a trip to Korea. Three generations of women drove down toward the sea to a place called Land's End. Along the way, grandma casually mentioned that her own grandfather was a hero of the Korean resistance to Japanese occupation. When he was twenty years old, he was captured and tortured, and returned unbroken but destitute. Years later, when we were free of one occupation and about to be yoked under another, the Korean government gave him a pension and a house in recognition for his bravery and service. The house, now grandma's inheritance, will be turned into a museum. Umma and grandma chatted about the plans for the property, while I wondered how I never knew this story. I thought about all the stories of resistance and struggle that have captured me my whole life.

Was it in my blood? My slacker, resistance blood? (No such thing, K. would say. It's all in the brain. And anyway, the existence of a gene is not a guarantee of the expression of that gene.)

When it mattered, I couldn't resist to save even myself. I tell myself it would be different if I were fighting for someone else.

To One, a Pinhole

Sometimes K. was like you, but more annoying. Or rather, he was like the perception I had in my head of you as a little boy: always looking for the next fun thing, never able to sit still. (It is a perception that didn't grow in pace with the real you, a thoughtful, mature boy when you wanted to be.)

"We're twenty-two years old on a Friday night, and this is what we're doing? Playing chess?"

"It was your idea. And I'm twenty-one."

"We should be out! We should be experiencing things."

"I don't disagree with you."

I do disagree with him. K.'s constant itch for something else, something better, made me insecure and more than a little annoyed.

"Do you have any cash on you?"

"A bit. What do you need?"

"Let's get a six-pack of beers. I know a really good place to climb and sit. We don't even need a six-pack. Just a beer each."

"Sure, let's go. Can I borrow a sweater?"

"Yeah, of course. But this place, it's not so stable. If you put your foot the wrong way, it could go right through the wood."

"How fun. Let's go."

The two beers do not quite fit into the small brown paper bag they give us, so he zips them under his coat. "We're going to the fields we passed the other day. We have to be quiet, though. There is usually a guard next to the practice fields."

I grab my keys to stop them from jingling. We glide across the night-time grass, over the chain-link fence to a tall, dark tower of metal and wood scaffolding behind an old scoreboard.

"There's a ladder here. You climb up the ladder, like so. Now, when you get up here, you pull yourself through here"—he pulls himself through—"but keep your foot on this metal bar, always. Don't put all your weight on your left foot as you are pulling your right foot in. You could go right through the wood."

Up. Hands and feet and hands and feet. Ignore gravity; it is nothing but fear.

"You got this. You're fine. Remember to stay on the metal bars. And then you sit down and put your feet there. Don't you feel accomplished?"

"I do. It's nice up here."

"And now you get a beer as a reward. Cheers."

I take the bottle he offers me. "Cheers."

"Too much noise. I wish there were fewer cars. You get so used to ambient noise."

"I always wanted to be in the middle of the desert. Roaring silence."

He cranes his neck up to the sky. "I wish it were a bit clearer out."

"The moon is nice. But not many stars."

"I found some over here. Can't really see them, though. I wish it were like Iceland. So many stars."

"I remember. I have never seen so many stars. Ever."

He turns to me, his legs swinging aimlessly. "How's your grandmother doing?"

"She's all right. She gets confused easily, especially about whether she's here or in Korea. She keeps asking when I'm coming home."

"But she remembers you who are and everything?"

I nod. "She remembers people. But she's begun to make up stories that she believes really happened. She's doing all right, though."

"Do you want to climb down? Lie on the fields for a bit?"

"Yes. But I want to finish my beer first. Do you think I can throw this down? Will it break?"

"Not on the grass. Here on the side where there are rocks—"

Crash.

"You broke it! I'm going to drop mine."

"It won't break."

The impact is hollow, muffled, soft.

We climb down and lay on the grass head to head, looking up at the sky.

"Do you hear that? The jingling."

"Maybe it's someone's keys?"

"No, I don't think so. It's too constant. See, there it is again." I pop my head up and look around, but see nothing.

"If it doesn't belong to you or me, it doesn't matter."

I lay my head back down. "I am so comfortable. I could fall asleep here."

K. points to the sky. "Look at those clouds. They look like they're about to attack the moon."

"A cotton ball fleet."

"There are too many. They are going to eat the moon. Here they come."

"A relentless onslaught. Oh, that cloud is black."

"That looks so cool. You can still kind of see it, though. The softglow."

"The softglow."

"It's standing its ground."

I arch my head back. "I'm upside down."

"You know, you can turn around and look."

"Yeah, but I'm upside down. It's like things are growing out of the sky. If I let go, I'll fall into the clouds. I want to eat a cloud."

"You know what's cool? Think of the moon as a hole in a dome. The only exit. It's the light outside."

"What's outside?"

"Just light. Bright light."

"White light."

"And the moon is the only way to get out."

"A pinhole."

"A pinhole."

22.08.1862 (Doctor) Gradus ad Parnassum

I discovered a forgotten piano in the old lounge at school once, when I was living in a house named after Antonio Machado, which you could never remember so you called it the Macho Man House.

The piano was a wooden upright with a bench that wobbled. I found a plastic chair and dragged it in front of the piano. Middle C. A-minor scale. The notes disagreed with each other. The piano had not been played or tuned in ages. The pedal had no effect on the keys and one of the B-flats was stuck. I played anyway. I was remembering how to walk. Bits and pieces came back to me. My ear remembered, then my fingers, then my mind. In a flash I could play it all. I was running.

I thought of nothing when I played. Words did not exist. The only letters I thought of were the notes, and they were purely sounds in my mind. I floated through time. The air swirled to meet me. My fingers ran away from my body. Nothing. Everything. Backward and forward through time.

Still, thoughts came creeping in, and I would forget what I was playing. I would try to remember the notes but nothing would click. Only when I stopped thinking would my hands take over.

The piano received everything I did not express and transformed it into waves of sound that cascaded around the dusty room and flitted out the window. Perhaps one day, the piano, heavy with the souls of all who had passed by, would sink under the weight of feeling and become silent, refusing to play ever more.

23 Pairs of Chromosomes

In case you were wondering, our family is at least 99.9 percent Korean.

K. and I were, as usual, hanging out and doing nothing. I remember sitting at the foot of his bed, trying to get some reading in, and he asks me out of nowhere:

"Would you ever get your DNA sequenced?"

"I don't know what that entails."

K. opens a website and points his monitor toward me. "They send you a package. You spit in the tubes they give you and send it back. They sequence your genome and they tell you what it looks like, what conditions you are at greater risk of developing for the diseases that have an identifiable or strongly correlated genetic locus."

"Hm."

"Would you want to know? I am debating it."

"I'm not sure. It would depend on how strong the percentage risk of something is, and if there is anything I could do about it."

"Well let's take an extreme case. Huntington's Disease has an identified genetic variant. Would you want to know that basically you were going to die by the time you were fifty-five? Or diabetes. If I were at greater risk for that, I might cut down on sugars. Being privy to this information might lead to a lifestyle change that might spare me a lot of trouble later on. Although with Huntington's, I am not sure. There's nothing that could be done. I might decide to use the rest of my time traveling the world."

Sometimes he just talks.

"I might, if I believed the results were reliable."

"They are fairly reliable. The key is not to misinterpret what they say. Just because you have a gene does not necessarily mean it will be expressed. They warn you not to misinterpret the results. They also tell you your ancestry, going way back. Who knows, I might have some Asian in me."

I laugh. "I'm pretty sure I know I have Asian in me."

"So what do you think?"

"If it's going to make you more anxious but provide no actionable steps, I would say don't do it."

Then again, I think about death all the time. There is a pretty high percentage risk of that and not much I can do it about it, so I'm not sure how I am qualified to give this advice.

I happen to get a discount code a month later for this service, and I do it. It asks me what my primary interest is in doing this, and I choose "I don't know." When I finally receive my results, I send K. my username and password in case he's curious. I vaguely wonder about having gifted all of my genetic data to a company that will surely package this and sell it against my own interests, but I can't be bothered to care.

The results tell me that, under the standard data model, I am 99.9 percent Korean and 0.1 percent unassigned. Under another, more conservative model, I am 54.2 percent Korean, which sounds about right, since I am 100 percent Korean when I'm surrounded by white people and 0 percent Korean when I'm in Korea.

According to their analysis of my genes: I can taste bitterness (indeed), I prefer salty to sweet (correct), I likely have no dimples (incorrect, as my dimples are the first thing Koreans notice about me), I likely do not have red hair (correct).

I am also less likely to be a deep sleeper. I don't ask K. if this is genetics or this is just me, because he will say they are one and the same.

I am more likely to develop Alzheimer's. I choose not to believe this, even as I see my future every time I talk to halmoni.

I do not learn why I spend most days wondering if I am real, or most nights panicking about not being real when I die.

24. On a scale of 1–10, what face do you feel?

I was at work when grandpa was brought to the hospital for the last time. Interning at a tech startup, indoctrinated in capitalism, hoping to land a permanent job offer, I thought working was the most important thing in the world. To make something of myself, the way appa had. To not squander his gifts to me, to prove that I was not the selfish, entitled, lazy child I suspected he believed I was.

Before grandpa was diagnosed with colorectal cancer, he had episodes where he would freeze up in severe pain and high fever, unable to move. For eight months, I beat the land speed record (in our Honda Odyssey minivan, the first car you and I both drove) to race him to the emergency room each time he has an episode. And each time, the doctors tell him it is only an infection, that he is fine, that we are overreacting. "Nobody has a pain level of ten. Take some aspirin. Eat bland foods." Grandma reads somewhere that it is good to eat beef liver, and she boils bowls and bowls of it until I tell her that this probably isn't very scientific.

I am frustrated each time they send us away with no answers. We finally bring him to a place where they take Asian patients seriously and they find a tumor. They remove it. Grandpa is in good spirits, walking the exact number of steps they recommend he walk each day for his rehab. After the nurses give him his morning painkillers, he leaves funny voicemails on grandma's phone in a slow, sleepy voice about what he ate that day and how she is the best person in the world. I book an inn for Easter Weekend so we can recover by the seaside like old Romans.

And then one morning I am working on some piece of code when grandma calls me from the hospital. Something is wrong. He is in pain.

Irritated but duty-bound, I run out. Weill Cornell, please. 68th and York Avenue. (Why isn't umma here? Because she is home taking care of halmoni instead of here with her own beloved father. Where are grandpa's other children, our aunts and uncles? Why am I alone?) Probably another false alarm. He just needs some medication.

When I arrive, I see an expression on his face that I have never seen before, and, blessedly, can never recall again.

Where is auntie, grandma? What happened? What did the doctor say?

Your aunt is downstairs. She is trying to look for parking because the hospital lot is full.

The doctor tells me that grandpa has severe internal bleeding, and probably sepsis, maybe a complication from the last operation. Somebody should have thought to take him off of blood thinners and forgot. Nothing registers except that grandpa is grasping my hand with his left hand, and grandma's hand with his right.

"I am so lucky to have my whole family around me. Now go back to work. Tell your boss I gave you permission to come play with me. But now you have to go back or you might be fired!" He chuckles through his tremendous pain.

This is the last conversation we have.

They wheel him out and, for some reason, I go back to work.

I never forgive myself.

He returns from the operation in a coma. Our parents fly in from Korea. You fly in from Chicago. Our aunt apparently found somewhere to park her car, because she is here, too.

"He will never wake up something something blah blah kidneys and blood all we can do is make him comfortable. He is DNR."

Can you put him on dialysis? What is the issue affecting consciousness? Tell me each and every option.

"It isn't going to help, young lady. There is nothing we can do."

Put him on dialysis.

"He isn't going to wake up, it won't matter."

Put him on dialysis.

They put him on dialysis when they realize umma and I have nothing but time and rage. Two days later, his eyes flutter open. He cannot speak, but he can nod and squeeze our hands.

"This is coincidental. We must inform you that this does not indicate long-term survival."

Get out.

Aunts and uncles crowd in, and one of our uncles snaps to his children: "You are learning Korean from now on." We hold a service at his bedside. A friend of the family comes and asks to perform a faith healing. We let him do as he will.

Umma and I try to devise a communication board, but it doesn't work. Instead, we sing to him, and I tell him over and over again how much I love him, and how I know that everything I am—my curiosity, my intelligence, my language—is from him. He nods to me and squeezes my hand. Once, faintly, I think I hear him say my name.

I wonder if he is afraid.

After twenty-four hours by his side, umma sends me to check on our car. You are already home for the night with appa. I tell her it isn't important, but she insists. When I return, he has gone, died facing the East River. He hasn't moved, but his face is no longer his face, his skin no longer his skin. A shell. I kiss his forehead and I hold grandma and I wonder how I so deeply failed him.

As the first grandchild, despite my failure of not being a son, I am tasked with giving the eulogy at a grand funeral attended by all of the church elders and the congregation.

(I remember running through our place in 이태원 when grandpa was there, before you were born. Or maybe just after. He scooped me up and took me to Lotte Tower right before a party, and my ears popped because we rode the elevator so high. I wanted balloons and a crown. But a boy's crown, not a girl's one. The saleswoman assured me that the girl's one was much prettier, but I think I did end up with the boy's one. I wanted a sword, too, but I don't remember if I got one.)

They choose to display him in an open casket. You and I are the first to see him. When we look inside, we do not see grandpa. We see a twisted, macabre, yellow caricature, a waxy death mask that even now I cannot fully recall because my mind has papered over those details.

You run outside, cursing and sobbing, one of the rare times I see you truly freak out. "They had ONE FUCKING JOB. What is wrong with them?"

It's okay, I tell you. It's not him. Don't look at him like this. Look at the picture we chose. Remember the last time we went to their house and helped them garden, and that time he spent all night helping you make that beautiful, shiny blue pinewood derby car. This is just a body, a shell. It is meaningless.

I don't know what I'm saying, although it seems to calm you down. Were the undertaker here, I would strangle him with my own hands.

We go inside and greet hundreds of people we don't know, and listen to an hour of Korean that means nothing to us. And then it is my turn, and umma warns me not to cry in front of all of these people. I apologize in Korean for giving the eulogy in English.

My grandparents often came to visit me in Massachusetts, where I went to high school. Despite the fact that it was a four hour drive each way, they made this trip with frequency and with love.

On one occasion, my grandma asked me to give them a tour, and I decided to take them to a museum that was showing a special exhibit on found objects. I told my grandpa not to expect much, to please tell me when he was bored, and that we could go have lunch whenever he wanted. This particular exhibit showcased an artist who made sculptures out of gears and other mechanical parts. They were, quite literally, piles of rusting junk. After the second room, I was already bored and was beginning to feel bad that I couldn't show my grandparents a better time after they had come all this way.

I looked over at my grandpa, and was surprised to see that he was enraptured. He began to explain to me all of the little parts, where they came from, what they were for. This one is from the sink of a navy ship. That valve is crucial to submarine pressure. Oh, look at this funny little man! His eyes are made out of watch gears. And so on, as we traversed through the whole museum. Every bit of metal held an important function in its former life, and was now reborn as art.

At the end, he thanked me for taking him to see such a fun exhibit. "This is the kind of stuff your grandpa loves," my grandma said. "It makes him so happy. This was perfect."

I have never forgotten how humbled and stunned I was that anyone could be that knowledgeable about, and take such pleasure in, gears and piping. I had brought them there with the lowest of expectations, convinced that it would be a waste of time for everyone. Instead, my grandpa reminded me of how much fun it is to be fascinated by the things we see and to feel beauty in knowing how something works.

When we are children, we view the world with wonder. Everything is shiny and new and mysterious. We are fascinated with pebbles and clouds and mechanical watches. As we grow older, we become accustomed to these things. Sincerity becomes weakness. Curiosity is a nuisance. The earnest are trespassers. As we age, we become cynical, and we lose respect for the genuine.

But my grandpa was never cynical. The rest of us grow tired as we age. My grandpa, as he approached eighty-one years of life on this earth, never saw dreariness. He only grew curiouser and curiouser, to the point where it often exasperated the rest of us. He asked questions about everything because he wanted to learn about everything.

When I bought him a new GPS, he insisted that his eldest son, my uncle, use both his old and his new GPS at the same time, in order to test how they differed, and which offered the most optimal route. He loved people and wanted to know everything—and I mean *everything*—about them. Within ten minutes of meeting you, my grandpa would know your entire life story. He would know your name, and the names of your children, and where you worked and how long you had worked there and why, and what your schedule was, and what you liked to eat best. If you even hinted that you spoke a language other than English or Korean, he would jump at the chance to practice his Tagalog or Spanish or German. His probing effusiveness with strangers was often a source of embarrassment for my grandma and for me, but, even as we begged him to stop, we were proud of his warmth.

My grandpa let me become who I am.

The last time I was able to have a real conversation with him, he was in a lot of pain. But what came out of him weren't cries or complaints. He spoke only of how lucky he was. "My entire family is here around me," he said, in wonder and in love. He thanked me for taking the time to come to the hospital from my office, and then shooed me off back to work. "Don't worry," he said. "Just go back to work. Give my apologies to your boss, tell him I gave you permission to come play. Now go back to work, or they'll fire you."

If I had known that was the last time he would speak to me, I wouldn't have gone to work. I would have insisted on staying by his side and holding his hand and trying, though inevitably failing, to express my tremendous love for him. I really, really loved my grandpa. But I went back to work because he wanted me to, because seeing me be industrious and successful made him even happier than having me by his side. He let me go. That was his last and his greatest gift to me: his insistence that I go on and live my life.

We go home and our aunt counts the money the mourners gave us. I search every shelf and box and book in the house for any memento of him, for any birthday card he had ever written to me. What if he found them one day and thought I had discarded them, forgotten about them? Why was I so ungrateful? What is wrong with me?

"No," umma tells me. "He would have been touched that you kept them all of this time."

I find a program from my high school graduation. On the front, his signature and the date are scribbled in pencil. Inside, my name is starred and underlined.

25. The American Dream

You could say appa (the one who wasn't a slacker, according to your essay) achieved the American Dream. He and halmoni and his sisters came with twenty-five dollars, and in two years bought a house. Halmoni still feared the communists, though. She said they were everywhere, that they might find her and drag her back.

Once, she heard someone talking about a person in Canada who could find people. She filled out a form with her name, her grandfather's name, her family members' names, and where they lived. A year later, a phone call came for her that asked for her by her maiden name. Nobody here calls her by that name, and she was afraid the North Koreans had found her. But it was the Canadian agency. Her brother was alive, and forty-five years after he had been taken, she found her family again. They agreed to try to meet every year.

The first time she was allowed to travel back to North Korea—just Korea when she knew it last—she brought a ton of cash with her to give to her siblings. Halmoni and her brother did not know each other's faces.

The next two times she visited, she was personally greeted by government officials who escorted her to the nicest hotel in Pyongyang. They loved her, which made umma wonder whether halmoni's siblings ever saw any of that money.

But then the dictator, on some whim or another, closed the borders. Even halmoni, an honored guest who had been let in a rare three years in a row, could no longer get in. She saved $10,000 to send to her sister and brother. She promised never to use this money and kept it hidden in her sewing machine. She used to keep other large sums of money in a fanny pack hidden under her clothes. She was ready to escape at a moment's notice, just in case.

Sometimes, halmoni would accuse umma of hiding her money or taking her things. It would become a whole ordeal, and we would have to search every room in the house, every pocket of every coat, until halmoni found the money safely tucked away in her pants. This happened even the last time she had a stroke. You were at Andover then, and I'm not sure we ever told you about it.

All she wanted to know was whether someone had taken her money. I think umma thought at first that halmoni was persecuting her to make her look bad. Appa had little patience for this, or for anything else at the time, and would explode. We realized only later that tau proteins had already begun to snarl halmoni's brain. A full-speed motorcycle couldn't destroy her mind, but the tissue of her brain was now its last, greatest enemy, the only one to triumph against itself.

26. Fe (Iron)

Appa told me once that, for their first date, he took umma to watch *The Killing Fields* in theaters.

The Killing Fields, if you don't remember, is a movie about the Khmer Rouge in Cambodia. I remember asking him: "Why on earth would that be a first date movie?"

"It's a very good movie! Academy Award winner."

"Yes, but it isn't very romantic. It's about *genocide*."

Umma cut in then: "Tell her what you wore, too."

"Twenty-six years ago, I picked your mom up in velour track pants, lime green bowling shoes, and a digital Casio watch. I looked so cool. She couldn't get enough of me."

He was the youngest of three siblings—two older sisters. She was the youngest of three siblings—two older brothers. Both with seamstress mothers and science-minded fathers. Two interlocking puzzle pieces. Epsilon Lyrae double-double.

What umma didn't realize on that first date was that with the family name came halmoni, the family matriarch, the iron-willed widow, the neck who controlled the head of the household. Appa's devotion to halmoni gave us a blueprint for family allegiance, even as umma's deference to him and to this indomitable woman blared a red warning of what my future would hold for me if I chose umma's path: bound to put the needs of others ahead of my own, to leave the home of our mother to take care of another.

**For nine hours,
and nine more,
and nine more . . .**

he walked through the thick darkness without turning, not even one glance backward.

> "He walked for twenty-seven hours?
> He should have called a cab, geez."

After the man's song, the Queen had said nothing to her husband or to the man. Instead, she had gazed into the distance for a long time, and then raised her arms, palms facing upward, and lowered them, palms facing downward. The garnets around her wrists glittered in the sunless light, and a wan rainbow bounced from the gems toward a smoky river in the distance.

The woman in the petaled wreath appeared.

The man saw his wife, beautiful and ghostly, ever a bride, shimmering in and out of the air like a trick of light. Forgetting himself before the gods, he cried out and tried to embrace her. But she had no tangible form under the earth, with her bones burned and buried in the world above. His fingers passed right through hers, and though her mouth opened, no sound came out. He turned back at the Queen, who looked at him but said nothing. The Queen turned her gaze to the silent shade, and finally, to her own husband.

Then the Queen turned back to the man and spoke.

"You may go, mortal. Your wife may choose to follow you. Or she may not. Only she can know."

The man bowed, but the Queen held up a hand.

"Don't look back, not until the sunlight warms her skin. Or else, even if she follows you, she will be lost to you forever, even in death. And you shall not find her, no matter how widely you search my realm once you arrive at my shores for good. Now go."

"Why? Why can't he look back at her?"

Because looking back instead of forward is what robs us of the joy of the present.

"Okay, Confucius. Gimme a present."

The man looked upon his wife for a long moment and then turned and walked away, playing his lyre to guide him through the darkness that stretched without end. To descend into the gloom was easy enough. To escape was to sing a different song altogether, one he hummed to himself and—he hoped—to her behind him.

He sang of their first meeting on the mountaintop, and the love that had grown between them each bright afternoon. He sang of how her devotion to her family and her easy laughter had been a balm to his soul after a quest dripping with bloodshed and betrayal. He sang of how, after they had exchanged wreaths and she had run down to her cottage, he had followed shortly after, bearing gifts. But when he found her again, her soul was already gone, leaving behind an alabaster shell curled on the ash-strewn earth, steps away from the wreckage of her home, crimson droplets falling from her slender ankle, tears still falling from her blank eyes.

He sang, too, of the life that stretched before them, dappled in light and color, far from this gray expanse. He sang of the cottage he imagined rebuilding for her, in the shadow of their mountain, looking over a sun-drenched field of heather and a brook of crisp, sweet water. They would lie on their backs in their meadow, looking up at the stars that burst across the velvet sky each night, basking in the glow of the fire and their bodies together. He would play the lyre for her and she would sing with him. They would fill the pasture with cows and sheep and goats and chickens and want for nothing. She would spin soft skeins of wool and weave them into tapestries that told the stories he sang to her. They would grasp at all that life had to offer them and grow old together, their forms softening and graying with age, but their spirits never dulling, perhaps surrounded by beautiful golden children.

As he sang of the forests and glens they would explore together and the people and creatures they would befriend, the darkness began to ebb. He saw the path before him leading not out of the green marble cave where he had entered, but into a grove of black poplar trees circling scorched and salted earth. His heart beat faster and his feet and fingers followed as he walked and sang in time with his quickening heart, eager to rejoin the living and anxious to see her face again. Surely, she had chosen to follow him rather than to remain in that gray gloom? Surely, she would still want to be his wife? If he could just see her face—

And he looked back.

> "He had ONE job."

And he saw nothing but bright air turned black and remembered:

Don't look back, not until the sunlight warms her skin.

He fell into the ruined soil and screamed.

> "Well, that was a bummer."

28. Remember

When our oldest cousin was little, he spent twenty-eight weeks in daycare at a Korean nursery, where he learned perfect, elegant Korean (which he has since forgotten) and a smattering of English (which he has since perfected, with bonus curses). Halmoni would pick him up in the afternoons and walk him home, and when they passed by a restaurant, he would say in English, "Delicious! That's a delicious!" When they saw foreigners in their fancy outfits, he would say to her, "I'm going to buy you clothes like that when I'm older."

Out of all our cousins, she spent the most time with him and with us. She sang us hymns and Korean folk songs from morning to night while she was cooking, while she listened to the radio, while she put us to sleep.

When our other cousin was born, he wasn't as good-looking as he is now. Appa, tactful as he is, made fun of him at our aunt's bedside, just after the birth. Auntie kept that with her, and when you were born, she said, "And he made fun of *my* son?"

As you grew older, you two began to look so alike. Very handsome, of course. Not funny-looking at all.

Before your extremely handsome self was born, when I was three or so, I would always want to walk to the zoo with halmoni. Whenever we went, I would beg her to wear this flower print dress with a huge flower belt. We walked all the time, in Korea, in the States, everywhere. Next to gardening, it was her favorite thing to do. We loved walking with her to McDonald's for breakfast, where she would get a black coffee and we would get hash browns. We took long walks around the cul-de-sac near our house, and she would point out the most meticulous lawns and gardens and asked which ones we liked best. She gave each one a grade.

Before umma left her job to spend more time with us, halmoni made us egg and cheese sandwiches every day to take to school for lunch. I loved them until I saw that the other children who didn't bring lunch got to have pizza. Once, I asked a girl if she wanted to trade lunches with me, not expecting her to agree, and she jumped at the chance. I realized then that she envied the egg and cheese sandwiches I had begun to bemoan, the hand-packed lunch she never got.

I don't know why I'm writing all of this down now. I think I just don't want anyone to forget how happy and loved we were.

Messier 29 . . .

is a star cluster in the constellation Cygnus, the swan. Can you see it?

> "No. I see blurry dots. What is this, a telescope for ants?"

Hang on, let me focus it again. There. In some tellings, Orpheus was turned into a swan after his death and reunited with his lyre, which is that constellation right above us. Eurydice, of course, doesn't get a constellation.

> "Did she want to come back? Did he ask?"

Who can know? He went with his lyre, overcome with grief, unable to think about anything else. Black poplars and salt, these are the elements of a tragedy. Or certainly, he thought it was. He looked back to find only a wisp in the air, not even ashes to mark his loss. Bring a shade to light, and you have only light. When the story is told, it's told with sadness. His music granted him an audience, but he failed the test. The gods are cruel, powers play tricks on you, there is always a catch. Grief, regret, anguish. The truest word for it is one that doesn't exist in language.

But maybe it was a lesson all along.

> "Don't count your chickens before they hatch."

I . . . guess that works. But I was thinking more along the lines of:

Don't look back.

It wasn't a test, but a lesson. A cruel one, to be sure, but how else would he have learned? Had he not gone, or had they refused him outright, he would have spent the rest of his days on a futile quest, searching for some solution, striving ever further. He would have spent the rest of his life as a shade, like her if not with her. But maybe that itself is the point. What is life but distraction? Grasping for what is out of reach?

No. They had to teach him the only way he would learn—through utter failure.

Don't look back.

Perhaps she was perfectly content where she was. And for him to suddenly appear, in his mortal anguish, and wrench her from her blessed twilight—how is he to know her haze wasn't pleasant?

The arrogance of men. Believing theirs is the only pain, a pain beyond consolation, beyond comprehension—a pain so important that all other considerations pale in comparison.

Did she want to come back?

Flash Forward: 30 Days

"My theory is, if you go thirty days wanting to kill yourself—a full, uninterrupted thirty days—without a single moment where you think, 'Well, this is okay, I can work with this,' then maybe you should just do it. But it has to be a full thirty days, beginning to end."

Bed 31

I did have a plan when I started this, both for this letter, or whatever this has become, and for myself. I had a timeline and everything.

But I got in my own way. A classic case of me being 'chronically early,' as you used to say when you were trying to make me feel better about something impulsive I did. (Or, if you were annoyed: 'Just *chill* for once and take your time.')

It begins with me waking up and hearing:

"You STUPID FUCKING CUNT."

(Me? Not me.)

"Have some respect, Chris. They're only trying to help."

"I disrespect stupidity is what I disrespect."

"We gave him two juiceboxes, I don't know why he's so angry."

Laughter. Nobody takes him seriously. What's to take seriously?

This is Psychiatric Emergency.

Flash Forward: 32 Years

It isn't time for this chapter yet.

33. Elohim

Life is a distraction. X, Y, Z. Everything is a problem to solve, to distract the brain. Reaching for these higher questions, the unreachable, and then what? Everybody is on a level playing field. Ten billion dollars to the Large Hadron Collider, and not to children. Why? There was some reason. Don't think about it. Happiness is the moment pain is removed from the body. The sublime. That's what they call the sublime. Don't think about it. I have to think about it. Why? Because I feel guilty not thinking about it. That's because you're thinking about it. Neural correlates to explain faith—faith is lessened.

No. 34. Attendre et espérer

Before we go forward, another memory.

You never liked [—]. You didn't tell me that in words, and you were polite enough to him, but it was clear to me that you, like everyone else, didn't get him. And you, like everyone else, were right.

K. didn't get him either, and he did tell me so, but only after it was too late. "It's like you built this prison for yourself. I don't understand why [—] had this hold over you, or why you were hung up on him."

I remember drawing a smiley face on the rail of his balcony with the stub of his cigarette so I don't have to look at him while I try to gather my thoughts. "I can't explain it. For a long time, I regretted everything from last year. I wanted it to never have happened. But I did learn how terrible it can be to become lost in someone. I don't even know if it was love. But I don't know how to give just part of me."

"If you had a chance to redo the year, would you do it?"

"I thought for a long time that I would. I wished I had never met [—]. I still wish that. But looking back now, I don't think I would turn back time. There is so much time I spent with you, with G., with C., that I wouldn't give back. Our trip to Iceland cleared my head. So it's less that I would want to redo the year so much as I would want to delete [—] from it. Because at the time, my mind was so fogged over that I couldn't appreciate anything else, and, in retrospect, that was an enormous waste of my energy."

"I don't understand what it's like to have such extremes of feeling. I don't know, maybe there's something wrong with me. I've never had that."

"There's nothing wrong with you. You will, one day."

He says nothing. He is writing my name in ash.

35,904' 청계천

Heat. Haze. Humidity. Monsoon season unleashes a torrent of rain and mosquitoes. The smog envelops me. I don't remember what it's like to have a conversation in English. When the house is empty, I sit at the piano for hours.

When the house isn't empty, I go out. In the center of the city is a man-made stream, a project that transformed a sewage dump into a park. An artificial waterfall marks the beginning of the stream and a set of granite stairs leads from the street down to a path next to the water itself.

I descend.

The air is cooler next to the water. The stream is studded every so often with stone steps that cross to the other side. I begin to walk along the water. It is calm. Sometimes glass, sometimes opal. The white granite banks shimmer in the light and dazzle my eyes. I pass through a tunnel and disappear into the fetid darkness. The air grows danker and cooler, but heavier somehow. The dark stone drips with a film of condensation. A drop falls on my hair and trickles to my forehead, down my cheek. I feel nothing. I see nothing. I walk.

As I pass out of the tunnel, yellow-green tangles wave at me. Reeds have been planted along the water, perhaps to hide the artifice of the stream. Behind the mess of life, high stone walls obscure the city. Trumpet vines crawl up the walls and weeds shoot up through the cracks where the walls and the path meet. Left unchecked, the vines will cover the stone entirely.

The walkway is crowded, as it always is during the day, but I notice nothing but water and sky. I walk alone. I am a shade, a glimmer in the fog, a trick of light. I do not exist to these strangers, and they do not exist to me.

The reeds become wilder, unruly. Twilight storms. The rage of the sky has trampled on all of the green. Branches and leaves lay matted and clumped in the water. The water rushes faster now, and louder. White-caps foam on the current coursing past the stepping stones. The depths are ever-changing, green and blue and gray and black.

I walk in shadow again, under a bridge. The stream is wider here. No life, only stone stairs leading down to the water. No more stepping stones. Figures sit on the granite steps and stare across the water to the other bank. The light bounces on the water and dazes my eyes until the figures are no more than black shapes, floating, immobile.

I am in open air again. Feathery, light pink leaflets from Persian silk trees float down to tickle my arm. Irises join the reeds by the water and a willow weeps overhead.

The light is bright and blinding, but gray. Always gray. This is a world of gray and green. This haze refuses to be ignored or forgotten. Bright as it is, no true sun reaches here. Life grows only in shadow and cloud. The hot gold of the sun is long forgotten, left in another country in another time. I can barely remember it, and how can I miss something I do not remember?

Along the wall to my left, a ceramic mural cuts into the stone. Painted warriors on horses ride past me in the traditional colors of red and blue. I catch a glimpse of a sign as I walked past: *Soldiers bearing flags of the blue dragon, white tiger, god of the sun, and god of the moon are at the front, followed by a band of playing trumpets, bara ...*

The water is calmer now, nearly still. A breeze floats through my hair and the light does not hurt my eyes. I focus on the waving leaves, the gurgling water. There are no other sounds. I am free of my body and float only in my sensations.

Incident Report #36030
(Six More Sentences)

2:31 a.m. Cross of P. and L. Female, unconscious on sidewalk. Possibly intoxicated. Clothes and bag covered in vomit. EMS taking her in.

BA 37. Death Mask

We are getting there soon. But first.

As I've grown older, I've lost my language. The words rattle around in my head, but only in traces. When I was younger, I was annoyed that halmoni seemed to only want to talk to me when I was watching television or in the middle of a book or writing some silly story. She would sit down next to me on the sofa just as something was happening on the screen. She paid no attention to it.

"Granddaughter," she would begin.

And then she would talk about something she'd seen on the news, something terrible or beautiful, or she would talk about God.

But mostly, she would talk about death.

She wanted to die, she said. She was waiting for God to call her, to end her miserable existence. She had her clothes all picked out for that day. God would tell her when, and she would be ready. Happy. And when that day came, she would need a photograph. She wanted me to take her death portrait.

I tried to ignore her. I didn't understand how she could want to die, when the terror of death kept me up at night. I didn't understand why she had to say this to me while I was trying to watch television. I didn't understand why she had to say this to me at all. I was six, eight, ten, thirteen. How could I possibly be the right person to talk to?

(Yes, what kind of person would keep telling someone they loved how they didn't want to live anymore, and it was time to die? Who would do such a thing?

I'm sorry.)

I didn't know what to say, and even if I had known, I would have had no way of saying it. Already, I was losing my words. So I would smile and say no, halmoni, you aren't even old, nobody is dying, and I would change the subject. Eventually, she would get up and go to the kitchen or back to her room. Then I would cry out in terror, frustration, despair. I would occupy myself with stories about the underworld and the afterlife to try to understand. I returned again and again to Persephone and Hades, Eurydice and Orpheus, *Embracing the Light*, the Book of Revelation.

Umma told me later that this was the accident. I said I didn't think so, that she was just like this, that this ran in her side of the family. Some defect in the survival instinct. No, umma said, it was definitely the accident. Halmoni was never herself after that.

Mind? Matter?

One afternoon, when we were lounging in your room, appa asked us where our family would be in ten years. You were pretty young, although not a baby anymore. Appa was in his pajamas, lying on your bed with one arm behind his head, the other playing idly with one of your racecars. Or so my memory tells me.

And I replied: "I'm going to go to Harvard and become a writer, and M. is going to be in high school, and you and mommy will be working, and halmoni will be dead."

(Wrong, right, half-right, wrong.)

In that moment, I know I have said the wrong thing, but ten years sounds like a long time. I play tug of war with you over our favorite yellow blanket and I avoid looking at appa's face as he says:

"She won't be dead. She will be the empress, and you will take care of her after you go to law school and become a lawyer."

"Oh. Okay."

But that task didn't fall to me, or to either of her daughters, or to appa, with whom she lived all her life. Instead, umma, leaving her own parents to be a good wife and daughter-in-law and mother, has devoted almost two decades to managing halmoni's medications, singing songs with her, changing her diapers when she could no longer walk to the bathroom, feeding her soft porridge when she could no longer lift her hands, connecting an IV when she could no longer swallow porridge. Silent, seething, soothing, suffering service.

I did take halmoni's picture, once, before she began to dissolve. It was right around the time I took those pictures of you in a black trench coat with sunglasses and two BB guns, pretending you were in *The Matrix*.

Halmoni dressed herself in her very best 한복 and led me outside to the garden we had in our first apartment in Korea. There, framed by a million green leaves, dressed in pale violet and gray silk, she stood with a faint smile on her face. She kept retying the dark red sash high around her waist before each shot. I showed her each photograph one by one before I erased them.

Or so I remembered. I found later that I didn't erase all of them. They still exist, waiting. Every morning now when we try to feed her and she shakes her head, I wonder if we are being cruel and she wants to go. I wonder if I should edit the lighting on the photographs so they are ready to be framed. I've included them in this folder I've created for you in my computer.

38th Parallel. Remember . . . ?

She begins to tell strange stories. Stories that never happened, and not the kind that tell the truth.

She was at Pearl Harbor when they attacked. She was eating a banana, and she hasn't eaten a banana since then.

(She was still in Korea at the time, before there were two Koreas. I'm fairly certain we've seen her eating a banana, although now I can't be sure.)

She was in the hospital room when my cousin's son was born.

(She was at home with me.)

She went shopping with her friend.

(Her friend has been dead for years.)

She moved her husband's grave. She secretly exhumed it from its place in Korea and had it moved to my aunt's yard in New York.

(This gave me a chill when she said it, but I know his grave is still there. I know this because tomorrow, appa plans to exhume it for cremation, so that when she does pass, they can be together.)

But these events are clear in her memory. How can I convince her that these things never happened? She remembers them the way I remember watching her disappear up the hill and collide with a motorbike. Her anger is real when she speaks of slights she has suffered. Her joy is palpable when she tells me how much fun she had with her friend walking around the marketplace.

I could ask her questions, begin poking holes in her story, but why?

For now, I rejoice every time she calls me by my name.

3:09 a.m. February (When)

There is a tree. She may have stumbled against it.

Everything is yellow.

And then it is dark.

She is clutching her piano books. Chopin Ballades and Chopin Nocturnes. There is a gurney. She is not at the tree anymore. Light. More light. A whiter light. A brighter light.

—Name. Birthdate. Are you cold?

Yes.

—Why are you crying? Are you in pain?

It is dark.

—Blow into this, we need your blood pressure. Too low. Why are you crying? Oh. That is terrible. I am sorry. I am so sorry. Have you talked to anyone about this? That must have been very difficult.

It was. It is. It has been. But she is going to be okay.

—Yes, you are.

It is February now. February.

—No, it is not February. Is that when it happened?

February. It is February now.

It is dark.

—Blow. Blood pressure. Too low. Again.

Her blood pressure is naturally low.

—Let's try it again. Blood pressure. That's better.

Bag. Vomit, yes. Phone, wallet, keys: no. His number is here though, somewhere. She knows it is. She finds it.

It is dark.

6:54 a.m. She has the number. She must memorize it.

It is dark.

—Blow. Blood pressure. Do you remember what happened?

103

She does not.

—What happened to your face?

Her face? Chin: scratched and bruised. She tastes blood in her mouth. Her jaw will not open all the way.

She must have fallen.

—Do you remember anything that happened?

She was at her friend's house and she was walking home. Then she woke up crying in the ER.

—Do you know where you are?

The hospital.

—Do you know what day it is?

Saturday.

—The date?

Yes. It is not February.

—All right. The nurse will be by again to take your blood pressure in a little bit.

What time is it?

—It's eleven in the morning.

She needs to use the telephone.

—The guard will take you.

She needs her bag.

—You can copy down the number, but you have to give your bag back to the nurse.

She has forgotten the number.

—You have the number you need? The phone is this way. Down the hall. Here's a chair.

is an optical double star in the constellation Ursa Major. That means they look like a pair of stars, but are unrelated. Unlike true binary stars, which orbit each other and are gravitationally bound. Do you see it?

> "They look like diamond earrings. Shiny. But Ursa Major doesn't look like a bear at all. More like a deformed aardvark. Or the squirrel from Ice Age."

I'll be sure to write Ptolemy a letter.

> "What do you think Eurydice wanted?"

Can we ever truly know what someone wants? Maybe she did want to come back. Maybe she did hope for him to find her. But his love couldn't bind her to this life. Maybe it's a different lesson entirely—that no love is enough to stem the tide of time. That in the end, we are each of us alone.

And what if the Queen had said to him:

"She may go, but you must stay."

Would he have stayed and let her go? Free to live her life dancing with the wind and the stars, without him?

I think not. For he could not bear to be alone.

> "Even though she's the one who died alone."

That's right.

In another story, another woman, Alcestis, called the best of wives, does choose to die in her husband's place. Her husband, favored by the god Apollo, was gifted a reprieve from Death if he could find someone, anyone, to volunteer in his place. The husband first begs his father and his mother. They refuse, though they are old and he is yet young, and he curses them. But they cling to life, the same as he does. They love life, the same as he does.

Faced with her husband's increasing desperation, and imminent separation one way or another, the best of wives volunteers to go in his place out of devotion and piety. Or maybe out of relief to honorably escape a husband who would send her to die for him. Indeed, even as he sends her to his death, he cries out that, if only he had the voice, he would journey to the underworld and sing to bring her back. Just like Orpheus, his fellow Argonaut.

"More like Ar-BRO-naut."

As he laments her, she hovers in uncertainty, καὶ ζῶσαν εἰπεῖν καὶ θανοῦσαν ἔστι σοι—both living and dead, you might say.

"That doesn't even make sense. How can someone be both living *and* dead?"

In a coma, perhaps.

Then the great hero Heracles—

"You mean Hercules?"

—bumbles into the husband's palace on her burial day and is received with the utmost hospitality despite the husband's grief for the wife he sent to his own doom. Heracles, in return for this hospitality, wrestles Death at the woman's tomb to set her free.

> "He wrestles Death? The concept of Death?"

The godly personification of death. And then—

> "How do you wrestle Death? Does he put Death in a big bear hug until Death agrees to let Alcestis be all living and no dead?"

. . . Basically, yes. Let's say he gives Death a big hug. And then Heracles, unasked, saves a veiled Alcestis from the fields of asphodel and returns her to her husband. The husband takes her by the wrist, an echo of their wedding procession.

And she says nothing.

> "Why not? I would have so many questions. Like, how dare you make me die and then decide never mind, *don't* die?"

The husband asks Heracles why she stands in silence—not bothering to ask her directly, of course—and Heracles tells him that she remains bound to the gods below and will remain silent for three days.

The story of Alcestis ends there.

> "What a weird story. Did *she* want to come back? Wait, let me guess. We cannot know."

Now you're getting it. Let's go back inside now, it's cold.

1-401. Saturday Morning

Are you putting the pieces together yet? These disparate strands dislocated in time? These fragments of memory and myth and mismemory? These retellings of the stories I used to tell you, complete with your silly interruptions?

Or, in other words (your words, probably), why can't I be straightforward for once in my life and just say what really happened?

I can try. Though I may not succeed, since my concept of straightforward may not be yours.

From the hospital, I called K.

"Hello?"

"It's me. Did I leave my phone at your house last night?"

"Oh, hey. I'm not sure, I haven't checked. I'm not home right now. What number are you dialing from? I didn't know you had a 401 number."

"Where are you?"

"I am on my way to the bank, and then I have to go back to the lab."

"So you haven't seen my phone?"

"No, I'm sorry."

"Okay. I'll talk to you in a bit, then. I'm at the hospital."

"What?"

"I woke up in the ER."

"What? What happened?"

"I don't remember. I'm fine, though, don't worry."

"Which hospital?"

"I'm not sure. The general one, probably."

"Okay, hold on. I'm coming."

"Don't come. I'm fine, I swear. I just wanted to know if you had my phone."

"I'll be there soon. Do you know what wing you are in?"

"I have no idea. The rooms all begin with L, but that's it. Don't come. I am fine."

"I will be there soon."

"Wai—"

"It's all just a distraction. Everybody is on a level playing field. The more problems you have, the more distracted you are from the realization that everything is futile. That you can't ever know. And if you can, then what? What would you do? Exactly."

4:3. Ennui/Offui

Do you know what it's like to want to do nothing? Or worse, to want to do something, but everything worth doing is exhausting or joyless?

I don't mean those days when you were recovering from a hangover after partying too hard in K-town, or when you were cramming for midterms and you needed a day or two to sleep in.

I mean endless stretches of being unable to get out of bed, even to get a drink of water. Staring at my piano, less than an arm's length away, thinking about how much I like to play piano but unable to reach out and touch a single key. Starting a book and reading paragraphs and paragraphs without comprehending a single word. Watching startling amounts of old television, the same shows, the same episodes, in an unbroken loop, because my mind cannot process anything else.

I am so empty that even the terror of death has dissipated, leaving in its place a flat void.

And when I do get up, it feels—physically, I mean—like I am wearing a backpack filled with sand. Or lead. Whichever is denser. And so I lie back down. Sometimes on the floor, if somehow I've inched too far astray from my bed.

I thought for a long time that this was boredom. A strange kind of boredom that had me paralyzed in stasis while also jumping out of my mind in screaming frustration. Then, each time appa told me to get up and move around—*stop staring at that computer screen all day, it's bad for your eyes, did you even exercise today*—I thought it was laziness.

And maybe I am bored. And lazy. But there's something deeper here that is wrong with me, and I can't claw my way out of my head. Instead of looking forward, I keep looking back, like the man with the lyre, like that story of the pillar of salt.

44. Shade

You asked me once what Eurydice chose. But in the oldest sources we have, she doesn't get a choice, or a voice, or even a name.

Plato maintains that the gods never intended to give her back at all. When the so-called tragic hero sang his way underground, the gods presented him with a wraith, an illusion of her. Not because he looked back, or because he wanted her too much, or because his music was not enough, but because he did not love her enough to die. He journeyed below, but as a man alive. He came for her, but only on his own terms.

It was a punishment, not a lesson.

In this version, he is a coward who perverted the sacred underworld with the rattle of his still-present mortal breath. He would not let go of that feeble spark of human life in order to be one with his true love. Not like Alcestis, best of wives. And for that, says the philosopher, the ineffable gods refused him, tricked him, damned him.

Life is cowardice. Death is love.

Don't follow me.

4.5 stitches per inch

A few years ago, when we were all in the Catskills with halmoni and grandma and grandpa, and you went out fishing on the lake with grandpa and Lilly and appa, I asked halmoni to teach me how to knit. Since halmoni was already in the intermediate stages of dementia, umma didn't think she would be able to teach me anything.

I handed halmoni two needles and a skein of yarn. She took them up and scrutinized them through her gold-framed glasses.

"Knitting? You want to learn how to knit? Well, you have to start with the yarn here . . . now loop this part over the needle there . . . slip this one out . . . then back . . ."

And with that, halmoni started to knit the fastest scarf ever made. I sat, staring at her hands, trying to figure out what the hell she was doing.

Umma smirked. "I think she wanted you to *teach* her."

"I am teaching her." And halmoni kept on. Once in a while, she would look up with stern eyes. "Are you watching? Look at my hands. Now what do I do next, a front loop or back loop? No, a back loop. Pay attention."

You came in soon after with a bucket and laughed at the knot I was in until Lilly shook water all over you. Grandpa and grandma made stew from the fish you caught, and I made you wear my yarn tangle as a hat.

Hold that image in your mind, all of us together around the dinner table in that cabin, Lilly snuffling at our feet for food, nobody missing from our quincunx, and grandma and grandpa with us as a bonus. Reflect the warmth of that day back to umma and appa when the house feels emptiest.

BA 46. Phantom Limb

I had a dream last night that you were here. You didn't think anything had changed. But I wouldn't go with you, even if it made me sad, just a tiny bit.

But you didn't have your face. Your face was somebody else's.

I can't remember you.

4? 7?

—Yes? Do you need something?

When can she go home?

—The nurse can tell you that.

And where is she?

—I'll send for her.

Linoleum floor. Curtains for doors. Beds on wheels. The light is yellow. It is sickly.

—Do you know why you are here?

She fell because she drank too much, probably.

—The doctor needs to have a look at you so you can get an evaluation.

When will that be?

—There's a process. It's a busy day. It's going to be a while.

How long is a while?

—It's going to be a while.

When the curtain falls, she is not bored. Why isn't she bored? Sitting, lying, sitting, sitting all day waiting and waiting and waiting and waiting but she isn't bored. Nothing in her head, but she isn't bored.

—Blow. Blood pressure. Are you hurt?

Her head hurts, and her chin.

—On a scale of one to ten, how bad is the pain?

Four? Seven? She has no frame of reference for their scale.

—Do you want an aspirin or something?

Just some water, please.

—With ice?

Yes please.

She drinks and she drinks and she drinks, but her mouth is dry and full of ash.

48. Cadmium

K. arrives at the hospital about thirty minutes after I call, or approximately nine years in hospital time. A nurse ushers him in, and he sits next to me.

Of course, my first instinct is to apologize. "I'm sorry, you didn't have to come."

"What happened? Do you remember anything?"

"Not a lot."

"I'm not even going to ask if you're okay." He stands up and moves to the chair.

"I'm all right. Confused. Bored. I want to go home."

"What happened?"

"I don't know. I left your house, and I guess I must have fallen down. I woke up in the ER crying with vomit all over my clothes. I've been in and out since then."

"Why did you leave?"

"I don't remember. I should have stayed."

"I'm sorry. I should have walked you home."

He is the Bohr to my Heisenberg, my own walking lump of cadmium to steady my reactivity. (I don't think you read the copy of *Copenhagen* I gave you. You would like it, it's a play about physics.)

"No, it's not your fault. I drank too much."

He gets up from the chair and sits next to me again. "Okay, so you were drunk, you fell, you woke up here. Fine, okay. My question is: what is this place? Why won't they let you leave?"

"I have no idea. They said something about an evaluation."

"An evaluation? What kind of evaluation?"

"Not a clue. But I think there are a bunch of people before me."

"I see." He goes to the chair again.

"Yeah, I don't know. I just want to go home."

"You don't remember anything else?"

"No, nothing. Just waking up here."

"Are you cold?"

"I guess, a little."

"Here." He drapes a blanket over my shoulders.

"Thanks."

"So you have no idea when they will let you leave?"

"Nope. They won't tell me anything. Just that I have to be evaluated."

He picks up a sheet of paper from the bed and smiles at the digits I scribbled in haste.

"Yeah, I had to get your number from my bag and copy it down. They won't let me keep my bag or anything in it."

"Are you serious? Why not?"

"Yep. No idea."

He shakes his head.

"Hey. It's going to be okay." He draws me close, hand on the back of my head.

"I have to go. Just for a bit. I'll be back soon."

I watch him leave.

Dwelt a miner forty-niner
and his daughter Clementine

Halmoni loves that song. It's one of the only ones she still remembers, and I sing it to her because she is forgetting us now. Our conversations play out on a loop. The same questions again and again, as if each time they are born anew. As if they had never been born.

"When are you coming home?" she begins, when I call her.

"I'm not sure, I might be able to visit in June for a couple of weeks."

"June? I miss you so much, the house is so empty without you and your brother around."

"I miss you too, halmoni."

"When are you coming home?"

"June, halmoni."

"June? I miss you so much . . ."

Before she began to forget, I think she used to do this on purpose. She had no other way to reach me, so she asked me questions she knew the answers to, in order to keep me from slipping away. When I was young, I would ask her questions, too, the only way I knew how to converse in Korean. Like when I tried to ask her once what she was up to, but it came out as: "What are you doing?"

She happened to be in umma's closet at the time, putting away some clothes she had ironed and folded, and she heard an accusation. "What, did your mother put you up to this? I can't even go around in my own house?"

That night, umma was called into halmoni's room and nobody was happy and I didn't understand what I had done.

Appa asked us once what our family would be like if we were royals. I said, "I would be a princess and M. would be the joker and you would be the king and mommy would be the queen."

And then appa asked, "What about halmoni?"

And I said, "She would be the maid."

Appa reminded me, "No, she would be the grand empress." But halmoni was always cleaning and cooking and packing our lunches while umma and appa worked. I didn't say that part out loud, and appa fell asleep and we slipped away to play.

Now it is halmoni who slips away, bit by bit, word by word, tau protein by tau protein. Perhaps she is in her eternal sunshine. But perhaps she knows, somehow, that something isn't right.

How can anyone forget, and not care?

The Bible tells a different story. In this one, it is not his gaze that disintegrates her. Rather, it is her own glance back, on the wreckage and desolation of all she used to know, that ruins her.

The rule was simple:

Don't look back.

That was the only condition for salvation. But even as she ran away, she could not resist.

And so she became a pillar of salt. An offering to the gods. The curse of soil. A purifying agent. The preservation of all that was and is and ever will be.

—I'm going to be your nurse. We've just changed shifts.

Hello.

—You're here today because emergency medical services picked you up unconscious on the sidewalk and you were intoxicated. You also had a mixture of opiates and benzodiazepines in your system. You're lucky this wasn't worse.

Yes, she had a bit too much to drink last night. She forgot she had taken her prescribed medication earlier.

—Well, that's why you're at the hospital.

Yes.

—That's not the reason you're in this wing.

Oh. What is this wing?

—This is Psychiatric Emergency.

Psychiatric Emergency. Why is she here? It was an accident.

—You told us you had been raped a couple of days ago, but refused to have the police involved. That's why you're here.

She was raped, but not a couple of days ago.

—I see.

It happened back in February. And once before that, years ago, in November. But most recently in February. And last night she thought it was February.

—That makes more sense now.

She wasn't raped a couple of days ago. That didn't happen.

—We're going to do a CT scan of your skull, just to make sure your chin and jaw aren't fractured. The doctor will be in to evaluate you.

Okay. And when will that be?

—Unfortunately, I don't know how soon that will be. From what I can see, you're moving up in the list, but it'll probably be another couple of hours.

Thank you.

K. comes back an hour or two or twenty later. Time is a construct.

"How was your meeting?"

"It was good. How are you doing? Have they told you anything yet?"

"Not really. I got a CT scan for my face, to make sure nothing's broken or concussed."

"Your cheek is a bit bruised, too."

"I didn't notice."

He looks at me, then down, then at me again. "It's like you've retreated to this place inside your head and given up on your body. You have to take care of yourself."

I have nothing to say.

"Do you know when the doctor is going to see you yet?"

"No. They just keep telling me there are people he has to see ahead of me."

K. lifts the curtain. "Excuse me?"

"Can I help you?"

"Yes, may I speak with her nurse, please?"

"I'll go get her."

A nurse, not mine, comes by almost instantly. "Do you need something?"

"I was wondering, do you know when the doctor will come in to see her?"

"I don't know. It's a process. That's all I can tell you is—it's a process. Okay? There's a list fifty-two people long, and your friend has a couple of people ahead of her. It's just, it's a process. I'm sorry, but I really can't tell you when it will be. It will probably still be a while. It's just that it's a process."

"Okay. Thank you." K. lets the curtain fall. "So would you say that this will be a process?"

"I have been here forever. I'm really sorry you had to come."

"Nobody forced me to come. Have you met any interesting people here?"

"The guy in the corner goes to our school. I think he tried to commit suicide, because the doctor came in and said he has a lot to live for or something. His mom and friends are here."

"How do you know that?"

"I overheard them. Through these soundproof curtains."

"Yeah, what is up with these things? They could take them down and it wouldn't make a difference."

"You can hear everything. Oh, and across from us is this old guy, Chris. He's been here all day and keeps yelling about stuff. I don't even know what. Oh, there he goes again."

"What is he saying?"

"Not a clue. But he seems agitated."

"The guards seem to be pretty laid back about it."

"Yeah, they laugh at him. Before, one was like, 'We gave him two juice-boxes! I don't know why he's upset!'"

"Juiceboxes? Come on, man, you got juiceboxes. In fact, I could go for a juicebox right now."

"I had to have an armed escort the whole day."

"Are you serious?"

"A guy with a gun followed me all the way up as they wheeled me to the CT scan and back. For real."

"What do they think you're going to do?"

"I don't know. I wasn't thinking about attacking them, but having an armed escort made me want to throw a fire extinguisher at him."

"You're doing okay? I mean . . . you know."

"Yeah, I'm okay. I know why I'm in here now."

"Why?"

"Apparently all last night I thought it was February. I remember that, actually, raving about how it was February."

"So that's a crime? Just because you didn't know what month it was and got a little too drunk?"

"Well, not only that. Apparently, when they brought me in, I told them

I had been raped a couple of days ago. Which makes sense to me now, since I really thought it was February. But it's not. It's not February."

"I'm sorry, *what* happened in February?"

My voice is steady when I finally speak. "February is when [—] sodomized and videotaped me. It wasn't a drunk hookup that he didn't remember."

"Are you serious?"

I don't answer.

"I don't understand you at all. Not at all."

I finally look at him. "What do you mean?

"Nothing."

"Why do you say that?"

He doesn't answer.

53. Iodine

—How are you doing?

She is all right.

—Did they give you any disinfectant for those scratches?

Yes, she is fine.

—A couple of basic questions to start with, so we can get to know each other. Do you live here?

Yes.

—And do you live with anyone?

Yes, she lives with her roommate.

—Is that who is here with you today?

No, her roommate is not here.

—But she lives with you, so you won't be alone.

Yes, they get along just fine.

—Any history of mental illness in the family?

No.

—Cancer?

Not in her immediate family, no.

—Where does your family live?

They recently moved back to New York from Korea.

—Oh, that's nice. What does your father do?

He is the CEO of some company.

—And your mother?

She works at home. She used to be a banker.

—Have you had any health problems recently?

No.

—Do you do any illegal drugs?

No.

—Do you smoke?

No.

—Do you drink alcohol regularly?

She might have a drink with dinner once a week, with friends. This is unusual.

—Have you ever felt like harming yourself?

No.

—Any thoughts of suicide?

None.

—Do you know why you are here?

Yes, she drank too much last night and told the attendants she had been raped recently. This was because she thought it was February. It is not February.

—Did you know the person who sexually assaulted you?

Yes, she knows the person who raped her.

—Is he still around now?

No. She doesn't know where he is.

—I see. Did you seek any counseling after this happened?

Yes, once or twice during the semester and once over the summer. She did not find it helpful.

—Why not?

The therapist told her it was her fault for not resisting, and also implied that she was a whore for having sex outside of a committed relationship, because she told the therapist that she had been raped once before.

—Excuse me?

This is true. The-rapist. Looking back traditionally has not worked for her.

—Some people do not belong in this business. I take it you haven't gone back to seek counseling since then? Because the thing is, if you don't have someone to talk to, we should recommend some places for you.

She has an appointment on Monday.

—Oh, you do?

Yes.

—At what time?

Eleven in the morning.

—Well, that's good to hear. We will need to follow up with that, but

I'm glad you made an appointment. I hope this is more helpful than last time.

Yes, so does she.

—I need to write this up and make a phone call, but you should be discharged within the hour.

Thank you.

Six by Nine
(Not the Answer to Life,
the Universe, and Everything)

K. disappears again and returns as I am being discharged. "I borrowed a car. You shouldn't walk. We just have to fill up the gas on the way."

K. gives me his arm to steady me and his sweater to wear because all of my clothes are covered in vomit. My bag, too. My phone, wallet, and keys are missing. I never find them.

The car is sleek and compact, with a medallion of a lion on its front. We sit in silence for what feels like a while, even though the drive can't be that long.

"I thought we were going to stop at the gas station."

"Yeah, we'll go to the one down the street."

My fear of my own brain strikes again. "Do you think I'm overreacting?"

"No. If it happened as you say, then no. I don't think so."

"I wonder that a lot. I wonder if I made such a big deal out of it in my head and blew it out of proportion. Maybe that's just what happens. I don't know. I never know. I live in my head, and I don't know whether what I am remembering is real."

"I think it's different, for people who've experienced that once before."

"Experienced what?"

"That. People who've been . . . violated. Before. Since you said it happened to you your freshman year, too."

"Do you think I'm lying?"

"No. No, I don't think that at all."

"Can you teach me how to fill the tank? I've never done it before."

"Sure. You were both drunk?"

"Yeah. I mean, I understand that people make mistakes. There can be misunderstandings. But I was crying and yelling for him to stop, and—"

"He wouldn't."

"He wouldn't. All he said was that he would go slower. And it turns out he was recording it the whole time, which is just . . . "

"Did he have an excuse for that?"

"There is no excuse for that."

"You open the cap and put in the nozzle. Like so. Then you pump it until it stops. It'll stop automatically. There's a sensor."

"Oh, that's easy. And I won't set myself on fire or anything if my hands have static or something?"

"No, you won't set yourself on fire. Then you replace the cap, put this back, and you're done."

Five by Five

I called appa and umma a few days after I left the hospital, and I told them I had gotten really drunk and passed out on the way home and that's why they might get a sizable ER bill in the mail. None of which is a lie. Umma started to scold me and then appa made her put me on speakerphone so he could scream at me. He shouted that he wanted me to have fun, but that I shouldn't be so stupid if I wanted to get into law school, and I realized in that moment that he was proud and relieved underneath that anger, because he thought I was finally socializing like a normal college student who wasn't too introverted to have fun friends.

(Is that unfair? Maybe. More than anything, he wanted us to be okay, and he struggles with the concept that his okay and our okay might be different.)

I apologized and made sure the ER bill was sent to me instead, in case it said anything different from what I had led them to believe.

But I began this so I might explain to you why I planned to do what I did. And then I did it, in a different way than I intended, and it didn't work anyway, and here I am, writing to you as if you will read this when you never will.

But in any case, here it is:

Yes, I did drink too much.

Yes, I did wake up in the hospital thinking it was February.

No, it wasn't exactly an accident, although I didn't plan it for that specific moment.

No, I didn't forget I had also taken a lot of other pills that I had been saving for a while.

Why? The why is here, in these pages.

Yes, I was afraid.

No, I don't know if I am relieved that it didn't work.

And no.
I don't know if I will try again.

Messier 56. Swan Song of a Lyre.

The day after I call umma and appa about the hospital, K. sets up his worn, wooden chessboard on his glass living room table with deliberate care as I flop down on his sofa.

"That night. Did you talk about it with him after?"

"I did."

"What did he tell you?"

He holds two pawns behind his back, one in each fist, and holds them out to me.

I tap his left fist. Black. He turns the board and sits back in his chair. I take the pawn from his hand and station it with the others on my side.

"Lies. He swears he remembers nothing. But when I got up, I saw myself on his laptop screen. I found a video and deleted it from his computer, but I guess not well enough, because I found it back on his computer a couple of days later. He swore he didn't know how that happened."

"Right. Sure." He opens with a white pawn to d.4.

"I deleted his entire computer myself after that. All he kept saying was 'I'm so sorry, I'm so sorry, I hate myself, that's not me.' I'm like okay, that's not useful and also it literally is you." I mirror with a black pawn to d.5.

"Yeah." He has another pawn threaten mine. The Queen's Gambit.

"For the longest time, I wanted to know why. I kept asking him why he hated me. It drove me crazy. Then one day I didn't care anymore."

"Why he hated you? You think he hated you?"

"Yeah, I do." I mirror him again. Albin Countergambit.

"Why?"

"Because you wouldn't do that to someone unless you really hated them. Some deep anger, I don't know. You don't do that to someone you respect as a human being. I just wanted to know why he did it."

"I mean, I can tell you why." He takes one of my pawns, but I move my other pawn up a space instead of taking his. He sends another pawn to threaten my lone piece once again.

"Why?"

"He drank too much, probably."

"That's not a reason. Check."

He sees that my bishop is threatening his king, and he sends out his own bishop to protect it. "Being drunk makes people do crazy things."

"Lots of people get drunk, but they don't do *that*." I finally take one of his pawns, leaving him to take my bishop. With my bishop fallen and his to the side, our queens face each other across an open canal. Tempting. Threatening.

"Some people jump off buildings."

"I would rather he had. Check." I ignore the queens and take a front-line pawn with mine, endangering his king again.

"G. said he saw you guys." He has no choice but to move his king to get rid of my little pawn.

"He did. He passed the room as he was going back to his room, and I think the door was open." I take his queen with mine.

"Shit. I didn't see that. So G. was next door."

"I think he was asleep for most of it."

"Why didn't he do anything?"

"What do you mean?" I stare at him and accidentally knock one of the fallen white pawns off the table, but he's looking at the board.

"Well, you said you screamed, right?"

"I mean, yeah."

"So why didn't he do anything?"

"I don't know. Maybe he was asleep and didn't hear me. Or he thought it was something else. I don't know. I don't know."

"You're stronger than [—], though, right? Didn't you fight back?"

"I don't know. I pushed him off at one point, but he kept going. I don't know." I've lost the thread now, but I manage to castle, since he can't.

"Did anyone know you liked him? I mean, before we all moved into that apartment together. How did no one tell you this was a bad idea?"

"I don't know. You didn't say anything, either." I'm playing quickly now. Not so much out of instinct as it is haphazard whim.

"I didn't know. Would it have made a difference? If anyone had told you it was a bad idea."

"Probably not."

"Can I ask you something personal?"

"Since this has been such light conversation so far. Sure."

"Have you ever had an experience that wasn't like this?"

"No."

"So just those two times, and they were both . . . ?"

"I was seventeen my freshman year. I wasn't ready at all. And after that, I definitely wasn't ready. This was the first time I wanted it to happen with someone. And then, well."

He is mulling over another fallen rook. "You're one of the strongest people I know."

"I'm not. I'm just slow."

"What? No you're not."

"I am. I'm a sequential processor."

"A what?"

"It takes me a while to process one thing. And I have to process everything in order. So by the time I'm genuinely reacting to something big that's happened to me, a lot of time has passed. There's a delay. I do freak out eventually—you've seen me—but it takes me a while. And by then, I figure it's so long past that I might as well get over it."

"I don't buy that."

"It's true. That's also why people sometimes think I'm condescending."

"I guess you do sometimes have this air, like 'Oh, cool.' Like nothing really impresses you. I never know what you're thinking, or what you want."

The king is dead.

"Because I'm slow. When you see me react, I'm still trying to process things. I'm not trying to be enigmatic."

Here I am, processing. Maybe in about five years, if I'm still here, I'll have decided what to do with these words.

Messier 57. Ring Nebula

Write a life in six sentences.

I was born. I went to school. I was raped. I fell in love. I was raped again. I died (eventually, whether by my own hand or otherwise).

Is that my life?

There are certain moments in your life that your mind keeps traveling back to, like water circling a drain or the same corner of a coffee table always hitting your knee. At least, mine does. They aren't always big moments, or important ones, or the events that brought me here. Instead, I remember little things.

For example:

Umma and I were walking on an overpass in Seoul. We had bought this bag of huge rice crackers from a street vendor. Out of nowhere, she said, "Let's throw these on the cars!" So umma and I stood over a snarl of traffic and threw crackers into the air like frisbees. They fluttered onto windshields and exploded under wheels into bits of cream-colored dust that flew up with the grime of the city.

Or:

We were at a Mets game. Umma got box seats from her company every year, so she took my friend and me. She gave us white grapes to eat. You were too young to come. I was seven, maybe, and I only cared about the Yankees, and my friend didn't care about baseball at all, so we paid no attention to the game (although I do remember the Mets won that night). Instead, we picked the grapes off their stems and threw them at the spectators below until a middle-aged man looked up at us and began to shout. We hunkered down in our seats so he couldn't see us anymore and we laughed hysterically.

Or:

We were in California. I was five, and our cousin was seven. You were two years old and blinking curiously around the hotel room from umma's arms. Our room was on the fifth floor and had a balcony that looked over the entrance to the hotel. For some reason, our cousin and I had this idea to fill plastic Easter eggs with water and open them up over the passersby below. Crack—run away. Giggle. Crack—run away. The look of indignation and surprise on the faces that looked up only made us giggle more. Thus began my delinquent life of dropping things on people's heads.

But then I see a bright orange beanie. I smell the sour sweetness of a lime. And I cannot escape.

I could give you all of the gory, thrilling details. But they are irrelevant, and I don't write this to be cruel to you or to myself. What matters is that it happens over and over. When I swallow something the wrong way. When my hair gets caught in the door. When I wash the dishes. When I dress. When I undress. When I read the paper. When I don't read the paper.

The memory of my degradation does not degrade no matter how many times I access it. A malfunction of the glutamate receptors. It will not leave me. I haunt the sidewalk outside of the place we used to live. I stare up through the giant bay windows and imagine I can see into that same small, sparse room with the cheap blue sheets. I walk through places that hurt me. Nothing will disintegrate this memory, which is apparently stronger than all of the principles of psychology and neuroscience put together.

Sometimes, I wonder whether I will ever run into him again. I wonder if I can get him deported to a North Korean labor camp. I wonder if I can still be an abolitionist if I would make a carceral exception for him.

Writing this down allows me to look at myself as if from a distance. I will never see my face in the flesh. This mirror will have to do.

I write to remember. I write to forget.

This is how you forget and not care. When all that's worth remembering is what kills you.

58 Weeks Later
A Memorial to Young Womanhood
(or The Spirit of Youth)

Autumn. The air is crisp with the distinct smoky scent of fall. I never know what it is—the blaze of firewood in some happy backyard, perhaps. It reminds me of the smell of snow. The change always takes me by surprise. The trees are stubbornly green until one day, as if on schedule, the world burns orange.

Island of dirt in the middle of concrete. Iron benches appear every so often, the proud legacies of mysterious benefactors. In loving memory of Honey. To Irene Goldgarber, from her loving children and husband. In memory of Helene S. Chazan. To you, from us. This is where you lay down your burdens. I never do. At my feet fall drops of flame. I walk among them.

A slight hill in the trail leads me up. Where the flames have died, I walk on soft brown leather. Potpourri of toffee and pink calico. Up, far beyond reach, marigold knitted against brilliant blue. Pines here, oaks there, stray brambles all around. Hidden among the branches, a girl cast in bronze. Dark green, youthful, frozen in time, dress fluttering in some imaginary wind. Constance, my landmark. I keep my passage by these metal mementos. Time and street names hold no meaning.

Winding road from here to there—who put these curves here? This path is false. Constructed imperfections will never recreate nature. Too neat, too deliberate. The dirt is no less of an artifice than the roads to my sides, and the trees are not soundproof. There is no illusion. Everything is real. Solid. Loud. I am never alone. Still, it is a haven from speeding cars and lights.

Forward, always forward. In the planned chaos, one life strikes me. A slender trunk, a mess of branches reaching no higher than my head, an elegant disorder. The leaves are magenta and they flutter everywhere. They carpet the base of the tree in a perfect circle. A pond of vivid, rosy petals creating the illusion of reflection. An earthy mirror. It does not belong here, this tree. I cannot help reaching out to pluck a leaf from the disarray, but in my hand the glimmer disappears. Just a dead collection of dried-up cells.

The road ends, eventually. Past the ruined shell of a stone house, past the iron benches, past the massive tree trunk cut into a crude bench, the path stops. At its finish: a high circle of stone around an emerald. A garden of the dead. Name. Epitaph. Date endash date. The entirety of life contained in an accident of punctuation, an arbitrary designation of meaning to indicate separation.

Just another landmark. When the gates enter my vision, I turn around. I go on walking and don't look back.

BA 5/9. Darkness Visible

I am writing this out of habit now. I am not sure who will read this. Perhaps they will find it interesting, or annoying, or sad, or dumb.

I am lounging on K.'s balcony, watching the daylight ebb as the streetlamps take over. And K. begins in his usual way:

"Sometimes I wonder what we're all even doing."

"What do you mean?"

"Everyone is so concerned with the tiniest little things, their own problems, and they don't think to take a step back. We are on this tiny planet, this blue dot in a huge black space."

"No perspective?"

"No perspective. People focus so much on their lives. I do the same thing. What is it all for? Why do people have dreams?"

"To be fulfilled?"

"Okay, but then what? I simulate achieving all of my dreams, but there is nothing after that. So I get everything I want. And then what?"

"You enjoy it? Find something else? I don't know."

"We only do this to distract ourselves from the bigger question."

"Which is?"

"We are no closer to knowing what this is all for. It isn't in our concept. If you are on two planes, say X and Y, you can imagine a point within those dimensions. But you don't know what it is like to be three-dimensional. It isn't in your concept. A line doesn't know what it's like to be a cube."

"It's ineffable."

"Ineffable, right. Doesn't this stuff bother you?"

I stare at him. "Seriously? This is all I think about. My brain wants to jump out of my mind. Or my mind out of my brain. I start to panic. The thought of there being nothing else, only nothingness, bends my brain."

"We need these questions. We always need a problem to solve. Do you remember that argument I had with G. about the Large Hadron Collider? I still believe that."

"I don't remember. I don't think I was there."

"He asked me, 'Why spend ten billion dollars—ten *billion*—on the Large Hadron Collider and not give it to starving children?' And, okay, yes, starving children are awful, sad, all of that. Maybe it makes me an asshole. But our view is so limited. It's as important for us to try to find something more, to go beyond what we have now. There has to be something more than just existence. I need to know what it is. I think a lot of people do. I'm telling you, we need a revolution of the mind."

"I see what you're saying."

"If you think about it, everyone is born on the same playing field."

"Never mind, I don't see what you're saying. You're an idiot."

"No, hear me out. I really think everything balances out in the end."

"Is this your compensation theory thing again?"

"Sort of. People are born into different lots in life, that's true. But we all face the same questions. In a way, those people who have more problems to solve are more distracted. They don't think about this stuff as much, because they're too busy trying to figure out how to survive."

"I suppose there's an argument in that."

A stupid one.

"They think less about this than we do. Our problems, we should be thankful for them. That's what the brain does, it solves problems. Take depressed people, for example. They sit in their rooms, and they don't want to do anything. Why? Because the brain is trying to heal itself. It thinks, 'That's what I need to do.' The brain is good at that. Everything is problem-solving."

"But if everything is about solving problems, it is only about surviving."

"But that's all we do. What else is there? We try to survive. But why? What is it all for? What is the difference between being dead and alive?"

"Well in one of those scenarios, you are dead. I would say that is a significant difference from being not dead. The opposite, one might even say."

"No really, think about it. Death is a solution for some people. They can't take the pain anymore, so boom. There you go. In fact, I wonder how those people who think about this constantly can survive. Philosophers, for example. Everything is pointless. And they must know that. But I guess people don't kill themselves for that."

"I think that's the reason lots of people kill themselves. They can't see any purpose. The closest I came to killing myself was when I thought this was all completely pointless. But I didn't. Obviously. Because I'm terrified of death."

"I'm telling you, there is no real difference between being dead and alive. Death is nature's way of balancing everything out. Nothing beats entropy. You cannot win."

Is it too soon to joke that sometimes the things he says make me want to kill myself?

I shake my head. "But there has to be something after that. I have to believe there is a point. And that there is something more."

"But why do you believe that?"

"Because there is something beyond life than only our bodies."

"What does it mean to be alive? We can't reach anything. We just imitate everybody else. Go to school, get good grades, get a job, go to work. That is the way you survive, by not being an anomaly."

"But there is more to life than that."

"That's what we would like to believe. That's why we work toward solving these problems that will never have a solution."

"There *is* more than that. Being happy, loving someone, being a good person. I don't know."

"Do you know what happiness is? I don't think it's some state of being. It's a moment. The moment pain is removed from the body. That's when you're happy. It's a moment you have when you're out and the weather is nice and you're walking and you're okay. Nothing more." And he shrugs, as if he is saying the most normal thing in the world.

I am silent for a long time.

He looks at me. "You're really bothered by this."

"This is what keeps me awake at night. Every night before I go to sleep, I start to panic. Thinking about there being nothing, never having consciousness forever—*forever*. How can I imagine eternity? And then not existing for all of that?"

"Don't think about it."

"I have to!"

"Why? There's no solution."

"No, but I feel guilty not thinking about it. And then I can't breathe."

"That's because you're thinking about it. Soon enough you'll be distracted by something, and you'll forget about this. That's happiness."

"But if I don't think about it, and then I do, it's like I've wasted all of this time being so complacent in my daily life and ignoring what's important. All this time, I could have been looking for a solution. I know logically that I'm not going to find a solution. I'm not going to beat death or find a way to know what's going to happen. It's unavoidable. But I have to try."

I do understand the irony of saying this, after all of my futile plans. How can I explain this but to say that despair is both an eternity and but a passing moment? The terror of death that tormented me as a child has returned and filled me with morbid relief that I am once again too anxious to die.

"What if everything could be explained away? Even your faith in God, the afterlife, whatever. Say in forty or fifty years scientists find the neural correlates for faith. Then what? Doesn't that lessen faith?"

"That might explain why I have a tendency to believe in God, but that doesn't disprove that God exists. God existing is separate from whether or not my faith is real or imagined."

"Okay, that is true. But I'm not talking about that. Forget whether God exists or doesn't exist. Take the concept of the soul. You believe there is something other than your mind that lives beyond the body, and you think it's related to emotion and good and bad and faith and love and everything like that."

"Yes."

"But where is it? It has to be in the brain. And if they break down everything into neural correlates . . ."

"Oh. I see what you're saying. This is what you meant that other time when you were talking about the homunculus and Descartes or whatever."

"Exactly. So if they find that, those neural correlates, what would you say?"

"I could choose not to believe them."

"That's also a neural correlate."

"But there has to be more. I don't believe everything can be explained physically."

"What else is there? Until you can prove to me that it can be explained otherwise, this is what we have."

"You don't think there's something else? Like . . . emergence. Something besides neural action potentials that determines love, art, our existence? It doesn't bother you to think about not being conscious of yourself ever again? Of there being nothing?"

"What is nothing, though? We can't imagine that, either. Imagine nothing. What do you see? Darkness. But that's something."

"It's ineffable." I get up to stretch and look for my jacket.

"Right. Ineffable. Hold on a second, let me put on my shoes, I'll walk you home."

"It's one block."

"It's getting pretty late, I'll walk you. No problem. The nice thing about this is, in a moment we'll forget about it. At least I will."

"I won't. Do you enjoy giving me panic attacks?"

"You'll get distracted by something else, don't worry. And see, knowing that I am not alone in thinking this, that somebody else—that I can relate to you, and you can understand what I'm saying, or at least I think you can—I find that comforting. So thank you. I will sleep well tonight. Of course, you probably won't sleep at all."

Maybe I won't. But in writing this, I have remembered what anchors me to this life, despite the black hole of questions K. keeps opening up. For all of his disconcerting theories of the mind and the universe, there are things he cannot diminish with a smug wave of his neuroscientist hand—

—the gasping laughter that seized my ribs the time you snuck around corners pretending to assassinate me with a Motorola Razr that you had programmed to make gun noises

—the ease with which you sunnily disposed of my most morose moods when you came to visit me at school, making me wonder whether depression is even real and what was I so upset about, anyway

—the affection I felt that summer umma and appa put me on an all-lettuce diet when you showed me a secret stash of chocolate you kept for me in an alcove outside of your bedroom window

—the love and aggravation that ballooned in my chest every time you were so irresponsible that I wanted to scream at you for being such a brat, and at umma and appa for letting you get away with everything because you were their precious son, and in the same moment knowing that if anyone but me tried to come for you, I would murder them without blinking.

I shrug as I wave goodnight to K.

"I'll live."

Boethius

Oh, did you think that was the end?

History is a wheel.

6.0 Sentences, Again
(Five Years Later)

Write a life in six sentences.

Meet us at Marquee! Eeeeeeee what's uuuuuuuup wait shit I think I left my card at the bar hang on okay wait I think it's over there caaan we get another round, hey, do you have any updog? HAHAHA gotcha okay wait I gotta go, 76th and Broadway please hang on wait wait wait I'm good here, juss let me out here on the left okay thanks man have a good one. Mmm I'm hungry can I get nuggets please a lotta nuggets okay yum nuggets ooh, Bloomingdale's, no, they're closed, wait shit did I leave my wallet at McDonald's Siri call McDonald's wait my wallet's right here I am a GENIUS I'm gonna die a legend, Siri hang up. What are these fucking tarps books who reads books okay fuckers stop for me I'ma cross the street right here. Fuck.

Or, if you prefer something more clinical:

Preliminary on-scene investigation revealed the following: Vehicle #1 was traveling S/B on Broadway in the left lane just south of West 73rd Street. At the same time the pedestrian was walking northbound in the left lane of southbound Broadway. Vehicle #1 operator attempted to swerve to the right to avoid contact with the pedestrian but could not due to an uninvolved vehicle in the center lane. Vehicle #1 struck the pedestrian knocking him into the center median before falling to the pavement. The pedestrian was transported by EMS #42 to Weill Cornell Hospital for treatment. The pedestrian is listed as seriously injured and likely to die.

June 11, 4:Something AM.

I left the light on and the door unlocked, because I knew my brother would stumble in late, and I knew he would forget that he did, in fact, have a key in his wallet, because after a year of me nagging him, he finally made a copy of the apartment key, and sent me a picture of it. ("Aren't you proud of me?!?!")

I wake up to Lilly barking at the wall phone connected to the doorman downstairs.

"Police here for you. Can I send them up?"

Yes. Has he gotten himself arrested? Idiot.

There are two officers. No brother.

"Do you live here?"

Obviously.

"There's been an accident. Your brother was hit by a car. If you get your things together, we can give you a ride to the hospital. We'll be outside." One of them backs away when she sees Lilly, a yellow Labrador retriever who is afraid of her own shadow.

Is he all right? What condition is he in? What happened?

They were not the first responders, but he's alive and he's at the hospital. They'll take me right to him. They just need to verify my ID. Took them a little bit to find me because at first he was brought in as a John Doe.

I grab my laptop and my bag. I can do some bar exam study at his bedside. I hope his bones aren't too broken. I'm going to make fun of him so hard for this when he gets better. Maybe I should bring him some food. He brought me a sandwich and some orange juice when I was in the hospital a few weeks ago, right before my last law school exam.

One of them brings me into the ER.

"She is here to see M. She is his sister."

They point me to a curtain.

I see his legs. They look fine.

I see his head. Bloody. Eyes closed.

The doctor rubs his knuckles on my brother's sternum and a torn up arm twitches.

"That's good."

He's alive, he'll be fine. He just has to sleep it off.

"We're going to bring him to the Neuro ICU ward and do a bedside procedure to relieve the pressure. Bulb pressure craniotomy tube something something something."

I hear a low mutter about a Glasgow Scale score. They roll him out of my sight. I don't know where they're going.

"Are you family?"

Yes, I am his sister. Is he going to be okay?

"He's critical. Is there any other family here?"

My parents, but they're in Korea. Should I call them?

She doesn't even pause. "Yes. Call them."

I can't breathe.

6:20 a.m.

This waiting room will be my home for the next three months.

My parents are taking the next flight out of Seoul, but that won't get them here for another day. They call my aunt and uncle to come. My aunt admonishes me for not calling her sooner, then calls my cousins and yells at them for not picking up their phones right away.

This isn't helping.

A stream of doctors and nurses and procedures and time and his face is a disaster and his head is a disaster and his arm looks like the Beast after the wolves attacked him in the forest.

My friends show up at some point. More family. Not my soon-to-be fiancé, B., who is in Switzerland, and who does not get on the first flight back to New York.

6:30 p.m.

"Something something blah blah bilateral decompressive hemicraniectomy. This is a life-saving procedure. There are risks, and there is no guarantee that this will work or that this will bring him back. This is simply a life-saving procedure."

It isn't as if I had a choice. I sign the consent form with my parents on speakerphone.

We wait for hours.

He comes out with a deflated head. The procedure has stabilized the pressure a little bit. But not enough. The pressure in his head is too high, his blood pressure too low. I don't know where they put his skull, but they definitely don't sew it into his stomach.

I tell God I will fast from meat and dairy and eggs and eat only the bounty of his earth if he will return my brother to me. I tell him he can have my body and my voice and my soul and extinguish every trace of me despite my terror of eternal darkness.

I hear nothing.

My parents arrive, and I am not alone anymore. My father hands me an old neuroscience textbook and a student's *Gray's Anatomy* from back when I thought for thirty seconds that I might want to be a doctor, and I think he's kidding, and then I realize he's serious and he believes I can research our way out of this. I take the books, and I shake my head. For the first and only time in my entire life, I see my father cry.

Father's Day comes and I take him to lunch, but everything is pointless so I give up and eat a bit of meat and am I to blame for all of this? ὅρκους ἐγὼ γυναικὸς εἰς ὕδωρ γράφω—I write the oaths of a woman in water, because that is all mine are worth.

They do all sorts of things to my brother. Freeze him. Give him medicine. Withhold other medicine. At multiple points, they sit me down and tell me to prepare myself. But his body pulls through, and we grasp at Pandora's only gift.

64. Gadolinium Contrast Media

Hesiod tells us that a bronze anvil falling from the starry sky for nine nights and days would reach earth on the tenth, and again, that a bronze anvil falling through the earth nine nights and days would reach the depths of Tartarus on the tenth.

We are at the hospital every day.

We are not bored. Why aren't we bored? Sitting, lying, sitting, sitting all day waiting and waiting and waiting and waiting but we aren't bored. Nothing in our heads as we look at his, but we aren't bored.

We spend days obsessing over pupil sizes and brain scans and EEGs and what they could mean with relation to his something something areas in the brain. I used to know these things, but my glutamate receptors, it seems, have finally taken mercy on me. Rest. You don't need this information anymore. Forget that time.

I keep whispering in his ear to sleep it off. Sleep it off, wake up refreshed. When his eyes open for the first time and his arm twitches even without a sternal rub, I think all my prayers have been answered.

They haven't. His eyes are blank. His hands clench and he suddenly stretches out his arms and locks his elbows and widens his eyes and makes this face as if he's in pain and he gasps.

"Posturing. This is an indication of severe traumatic brain injury blah blah something blah."

In the moment, I soak up every word. I can repeat the words verbatim to my parents and break them down into normal language when I explain them to my family and friends. I research online and scan through the textbooks my father brought and read articles and ask K. to send me more articles.

But to reach back into that moment now is to scrape away at the thin membrane that stretches between my current state of mind and what lies beneath that blessed scab. I could go back and pinpoint exactly what they did and when and how, but why? It is meaningless, and my brain has dammed that time for a reason.

Imagine the bronze anvil falling even through Tartarus, into Night, into the primordial Chasm itself. It falls and it falls and I fall and it falls and even infinite abyss cannot contain my grief.

Messier 65. Spiral Galaxy in Leo

B. eventually comes back from Germany or Switzerland or wherever he was. He returns a week earlier than planned, "for you," he says, but the damage is done. A wall has grown between us, and I don't know how to dismantle it. Vinegar, maybe, like Hannibal crossing the Alps.

B. comes to the hospital with me and studies for the bar through earphones as I sit at my brother's bedside. When he looks up from his screen, he is ever positive, ever supportive, but the fraughtness of the moment gives rise to infinite interpretations of his behavior. My father circles him for a few days, a lion stalking prey, then forbids him from coming to the hospital or to my apartment ever again. "He never even told me sorry about my son." My father says he will let this go once we are married. B. doesn't understand what he did, but he stays away. I think of nothing but death as I stare at the television in the hospital room while the nurses change my brother's bandages and I wonder over and over why B. didn't find the first flight back to New York, why he can do nothing for me now.

K. flies in from Pasadena, where he lives with his fiancée. I send him all of the brain scans and he does something something Matlab something to the images on his computer. He explains the images to my parents in the calm, soothing, didactic way he has. So earnest, so eager for us to understand what he is saying. The calm-speaking German, as my brother used to call him.

("But he's Albanian," I would tell him.

"That's not a real country," my brother would answer serenely.)

June 6, 1987: D-Day

As the nurses wrap and rewrap my brother in fresh, sterile gauze night after night, I am reminded for some reason of a photograph of my mother on her wedding day. She wore a white satin dress with long, puffy sleeves, a gossamer veil with a flower crown, and a train to rival that of a princess. She and my father took their photographs at the Old Westbury Gardens, and their expressions in the images belie the disastrous atmosphere. It is too bright, too hot, my father's suit is too dark, there are seven hundred church members at this dry wedding, can't we get this over with?

They fly to Paris to begin a whirlwind thirteen-city journey through Europe with a tour group that is on exactly the precise schedule you might expect. My father insists that my mother packed seven suitcases with a different outfit for each night, and my mother says that my father is being ridiculous. When they get to the top of the Eiffel Tower, they are fighting (nobody remembers why), and my father won't share any of his French onion soup with her.

Ten years later, they bring my brother and my halmoni and me to Paris, and we stay in a beautiful, creaky room with wide windows looking out onto the Eiffel Tower. My mom says she will get a French onion soup and eat it all by herself. I drag my parents to every museum and garden, and for the next five years, I study French out of an outdated dictionary and tell everyone I will live in France. I dream about the hall of mirrors and keep the token my mother buys me from the Gardens of Versailles my whole life.

My brother's primary memory was playing 묵찌빠 on the metro and riding the merry-go-round and, on our last day in Paris, triumphantly convincing my parents to buy us the cotton candy we had been eyeing all week. I wonder if we wrapped my brother in cotton candy instead of gauze, he might wake up with a laugh.

*67. If youre [*sic*] reading this, its [*sic*] too late.

My brother loved Drake, which I found unfathomable. What a whiner. Listen to someone fun. Like Chance! You love Chance the Rapper.

"Drake should be president."

I find an old video of my brother in a pink Hotline Bling sweatshirt, imitating Drake exactly. I watch this video over and over again as I sit by his bedside, and I blast Drake for him even as I cringe through every confessional lyric. I read to him a poem by Chinaka Hodge called "Drake questions the deceased, Vegas," and I laugh to myself and then I start crying as I imagine my brother singing that if he dies, he's a legend.

Take me with you where you are. Let me be free of these sensations.

68. Greenberg 2 South West

My parents force me to leave the hospital. Go home. Take a shower. Sleep. Nothing is going to happen today.

The first time they say this, I go home and my father calls me back as soon as I get there. Come. Something is happening. Come now. I run out into the street with no bra and just the long t-shirt I threw on coming out of the shower and I desperately hail a cab. "Weill Cornell at 68th and York, please. Please, if you can go as quickly as you can. Please."
I sob silently, desperately, as I call my parents back again and again, trying to understand what is happening. They don't answer. How can so many cars be crossing the Central Park transverse at this exact time? The driver asks for my brother's name, and tells me he will pray for him. شكرا I whisper over my sobs.

My brother's heart has stopped. I walk in to see a tiny blonde nurse tirelessly performing CPR on him. My mother is weeping in the corner. My father is staring, his expression furious and helpless. Thirty minutes of compressions. My mother thinks it is this, and not the collision or the series of strokes, that destroys his brain.

His heart begins again. The crisis passes. They send me home again, and my father calls me back again. Another stroke. Oxygen is too low.

After that, I refuse to leave except when the surgeons order me out so they can operate on him yet again. The ICU monitor is my lullaby, the IV drip battery my alarm clock. I study for the bar exam between shift changes and pray to turn back time.

♋. June 21–July 22

My brother was born under Cancer, that twinkling crab in the night sky.

The Babylonians mention the crab in rites to raise spirits and to make offerings to the deceased. A crab in the liminal space between the living and the dead.

The Greeks say the goddess Hera sent a crab, Karkinos, to distract Heracles as he was battling the Lernean Hydra. Heracles crushed the crab with his foot without another thought. Hera sent the crab into the sky, deathless, eyeless, dark, forever.

His face is his face, and he looks at me with his eyes open, but they are blank. His face lies to me. If I don't look into his eyes, I think he could wake up and start laughing at me. "Why so serious? Stop studying, let's watch television."

But if there is only matter and no mind, he is already gone.

I imagine him dying under the foot of Heracles. I imagine his head crunching against the windshield and then the pavement.

Nothing matters. Every effort to stem my grief only makes it grow another roaring head.

Heracles, wrestle Death for me now and lead another soul out of asphodel. Remove this pain from my body and crush the Hydra living in my head.

Lucky Number 7

He was always a lucky boy. A happy, lucky, friendly boy. My father called him lucky boy, or sometimes MME, short for 멍멍이, Korean for dog. My brother always picked the number 7, but then started adding a 3 or a 33 in there, I think because of me. He was assigned a number 32 jersey once, which he traded with a teammate for a number 33—my number was always 33, and he wanted to be like me, when we were younger.

I don't think I lived up to his expectations.

He believed himself invincible. We all believed him invincible. I am writing this as I look at a picture of him petting our dog, and I think he will step out of the frame, laughing, asking me what I got him for his birthday, begging me to make him something to eat because he is hungry.

July 14

In honor of my brother's birthday, and my brother being moved from the ICU to the step-down unit, my father lifts the ban on B. coming to my apartment. B. isn't actually in town when my father makes the announcement, but he is happy about it. He makes plans for what we will do when he is back in August, the countries we will explore. He talks about the climbing trips he is planning for when he finishes taking the bar exam. I explain to him that I will have to cancel our bar trip, because I will be with my mother at my brother's bedside at the rehab center, which looks like it was last furnished in the seventies but at least is staffed by doctors who have time for our questions.

B. is unhappy about this. I am indifferent.

I walk through Central Park, and I stay with my mother and brother as he is moved from the step-down unit back to the ICU for a new pneumonia.

We bring cakes and juiceboxes for the nurses. I wish on his candles that he will be alive next year to celebrate another birthday.

72 Days After the Accident

As I await the results of yet another surgery, I get a text from K. "Are you free tonight?"

I tell K. I will let him know after the surgery. And for once, in this selfish, stifling summer of triaging relationships and messages and phone calls, I keep my promise. I send him a message letting him know the surgery went well and ask him whether he is still free tonight.

Hours later, he calls me. "Hey! Sorry, my phone was off. I got married today. We eloped."

"Fuck you."

"There will be a ceremony and you will definitely be invited. It was literally just us and my brother as our witness."

I witness my brother every day, but he will never witness me. "Does your mom know? Is she going to be pissed?"

"It's been kind of crazy. Yeah she is very, very upset."

"You idiot. I'm so, so happy for you. Congratulations! I think she's great." I think I sound pretty convincing and not like someone about to kill herself.

"I know; I am fucking insane."

"Your mom is going to murder you."

"I know."

"How long were you planning it?"

"We just wanted to do it. Want to come have a drink with us? If not, it's totally okay. I can see you tomorrow."

"I would, but I'm in my brother's room at the apartment and my father is sleeping in my room, which means I have no clothes but the pink squirrel pajamas I am wearing. I would not want to embarrass the newlyweds in public."

"Of course, of course. It really was just my brother there. I told my parents last night. We will definitely have a ceremony, probably sometime next spring."

"Yeah, yeah."

"Don't be mad! Let's hang out tomorrow if you're free. Text me about tomorrow."

"I will. Congratulations again."

73rd and Broadway

Despite the ICU's best efforts, I pass the bar with the highest score I know. In retrospect, all my studying seems a bit of a waste, since the exam is essentially pass/fail.

B. proposes to me the weekend before we start work at our law firm. Do you want to go for a walk, he asks. I am suspicious because he never wants to walk anywhere that he can bike. I know what he is planning. We take Lilly to Riverside Park, and he asks me if, despite everything, I think I can be a happy person. I lie and say yes and resent the fact that he has conditioned the proposal I know is coming on this deeply unfair and unanswerable question at the worst time in my life.

Do you want to get married, he asks. He brings out a ring pop. I say yes, and for a moment I really do, and fireworks explode over the river by pure happenstance. Lilly leaps up, startled, and tries to drag me home.

We walk home to take pictures and tell everyone and, on the way, I pass the accident site. The next day, a lawyer who takes pity on me sends me the police file on my brother's investigation that he received from a contact of his. It includes a security video of my brother's last moments awake. My father wants someone to watch it, to make sure no one needs to be sued. He wants to punish someone, but there is no one to punish.

I watch the video alone. My brother bobs and weaves up from the train station. He is eating something, I imagine chicken nuggets. He is happily drunk. Back and forth, back and forth, and then he walks through the tarp-covered bookstands that are always there, an illicit, beloved institution. He walks into the street, and he flies through the air.

I never allow my parents to watch this video.

There is a crack in the pavement next to the guardrail outside of the 72nd Street station, and I can't remember if that was already there, or whether it is the shape of my brother's body.

I descend into the station the next day to go to work.
I descend into the station every morning to go to work.
I descend into the station every morning and I die.

74 Days Later (Thanksgiving)

I am napping, and B. asks me if I am happy.

I am never happy. I go back to sleep.

He leaves the apartment. Meet me at Riverside later, he says as he leaves.

He jumps up the moment I arrive. "I can't be with someone who can't be happy."

I stare at him. My brother is in a coma. My family is destroyed. My life has turned inside out. My daily goal is bare survival so that I can be with my mother so that she can be with my brother. What is happy? You lost your father, and it devastated you. Why can't you understand me?

"I don't mean that you have to be happy right now, but I need to know that one day in the future you will be happy."

I'm not a fucking fortune-teller.

"I'm not sure we're ready to get married."

Fine. Give me back my key.

"Wait. We can work this out."

It would take all of my self-control not to destroy him in this moment. This seems like a lot of effort.

I methodically lay out every sin he has committed since the moment of the accident, including continuing on his climbing trip even as I watched the surgeons remove both skull plates from my brother's head. I tell him he fundamentally lacks empathy.

He cries. I lost my father to suicide. I can't watch you go through that. Maybe it's selfish, but I can't.

Fine. Go home. Think about what you want.

He comes back in the morning and tells me he loves me and wants to marry me and will stick with me through everything.

Okay.

I can't be bothered to make a decision either way, so I let him say we will put this all behind us and not look back.

Unit 7, 5 Peter Cooper Village.

I used to live below the happiest and saddest woman in the world.

I only saw her in person once, when I was on her floor hunting for a misplaced package. She was coming out of her apartment wearing a ruby red suit. She smiled at me, open and friendly, as she passed me by.

For the first six months, I heard laughter during the day and the vocal sounds of a couple becoming horizontally refreshed at night, always around two in the morning.

For the six months after that, day and night, I heard only the woman's sobs. Sometimes quiet and contained, sometimes anguished and shrieking. Always desperate.

I thought perhaps her paramour had left her, and it was time for her to move on. I wasn't annoyed, mainly curious and a little concerned about her emotional attachment to this mystery person who was clearly never coming back and did not deserve her grief.

In hindsight, as usual, I knew nothing.

The first time I returned to my apartment alone after the accident, I stepped into the shower and screamed. I thought I could expel my horror and terror and disbelief in one, primal, unhindered scream from the depths of my lungs.

I could not. I screamed and I screamed and I screamed and the Chasm inside of me only grew.

I wonder what that woman lost. Mostly, I wonder what my neighbors think of me every time I break down. To my eternal gratitude, I have never heard a word from them about it.

76th and Broadway

Even before the accident, I thought his room was haunted. Not really, because it probably isn't and ghosts probably aren't real, but his window would never stay shut. I would close it, and then hours later I would pass by and the top of it would be open again. Or sometimes the bottom would have lifted itself up. The room was always colder than the rest of the apartment, and sometimes I heard funny noises that I could never figure out.

His room really is haunted now, by the presence and absence of him. Every morning at 8:01, his Casio watch beeps from the mother-of-pearl chest drawer I placed it in after retrieving a hazardous materials bag of his broken and bloodied belongings from hospital security. He told me he once had a huge meeting and he set a bunch of alarms on his phone, and he slept through all of them and only woke up because he had accidentally set his watch alarm to 8:01. He said he was never turning the alarm off after that, just in case.

I expect him to come out of his room at any moment and demand that I stop studying and tell him a story instead. I remember him occupying the dining table chair and stealing my new headphones to listen to the *Lilo and Stitch* soundtrack. I trace every spot in the apartment where he wrestled Lilly and fed her biscuits and played ticklefoot with her.

("Stop tickling her foot with her tail."

"She likes it! It is her favorite game.")

I want to sell this apartment and never see the crack next to the train station again. But then some stranger will move in here and erase him, and I won't even have his ghost to keep me company.

Why did you come for him? I was right here. I would have volunteered.

7/11. American Dream, Redux

On my first day at my law firm, I had to explain to everybody that I was a bad investment.

I tell this to my extraordinarily accomplished Mentor, whom I think must have all the answers. I tell her about the accident, that now my brother is in a room at a rehab center that my mother has made into her home. Mentor assures me that people will understand, that I just need to speak to the right people and put a plan into place.

So I try to explain myself to the right people.

I cannot work weekends at the moment, and I cannot travel. My brother is in a coma, and I have to take care of him on the weekends. Please excuse any delay in response.

"We are so sorry. Please let us know if there is anything we can do."

Thank you.

"But once your situation changes, let us know; we may need you to fly out to help out with some witness interviews."

To be candid, I don't think I will be able to travel for a while.

"Yes, we understand. But maybe once things change. It'll be a good opportunity for you."

At this point, I don't see the situation changing until my brother dies.

"Of course. But when it does change, we can talk about travel."

Does this person realize what she is saying?

Somehow, though, I make it to the office every morning, and at the end of the night (or early the next morning), I have done something at least passably not incompetent. I can almost forget I have another life, a train taking me to despair every weekend, and instead focus on expanding that (illusory, predatory) American Dream.

And then I remember, and I lose all oxygen.

I wonder what I could accomplish if I didn't spend all of my energy carrying this trauma. Or maybe this is an excuse I use to avoid the possibility that perhaps I am simply mediocre.

I tell this to Mentor. She has no answers for me, and I realize she finds life as pointless as I do.

"My theory is, if you go thirty days wanting to kill yourself—a full, uninterrupted thirty days—without a single moment where you think, 'Well, this is okay, I can work with this,' then maybe you should just do it. But it has to be a full thirty days, beginning to end."

Her realistic nihilism comforts me.

I go thirty days, and then another thirty days, and then another, and I find myself still alive. Not because anything makes me feel okay, but out of fear and sheer force of will. I cannot leave my mother alone.

Each weekend, I sit at my brother's bedside and play him music and tell him about my day while my mother goes home to shower and sleep. We become experts in intubation and trachs and suction and EEGs and feeding tubes. My mother jokes that maybe he'll wake up if we feed him his beloved blue 7/11 Slurpee through his PEG. We can diagnose every cough, soothe every rash, heal any swelling, understand every guttural vocalization, every gurgle, every shade of urine, every posturing tremor he makes. I speak exclusively in jargon, because it is the only way the doctors take us seriously. They realize that we will always have follow-ups to their confident, empty answers, and they stop playing that game with us.

We can tell you the brand and generic names of every medication he takes or has on standby, and what his current dosage is, and when he received it last. We can tell you what to do if the first dosage doesn't kick in. We know the most efficient way of rolling his body one way, and then the other, to change him and to prevent bedsores without disturbing his soft, unprotected head. His body gains strength and we begin to think: we can do this. If we can just bring him home, even if he can't live the life he was meant to live, he can be comfortable.

We renovate our house. The French doors on the lower level lead straight out into a yard that overlooks a lake. My mother and I measure each wall and nook to see where we can install a bookshelf and a television, where the best place for his custom bed will be, how wide his accessible shower needs to be, what kind of showerheads it will need.

"Sometimes, I think I am being selfish. If he wakes up and he can't walk or do anything by himself, what kind of life is that?"

I don't know.

"But even if he won't be able to have the same life, he is still alive. I cannot let him go. How can I let him go? My baby boy? Look at his face. Doesn't he look like he will get up at any moment and call for me?"

He does.

I imagine him coming home and waking up to sunshine on his face. I wonder if one day he will smile. I wonder if he will speak, if the accident will change him, if he will tell me stories that never happened.

I wonder if he will be angry with us for pulling him back from where he was going.

I wonder if my mother will be by his side all her life.

I wonder if I will be by his side all his life.

I wonder if our lives are ours.

78. Shneim Asar Chodesh

I stop hoping B. will understand me, that he can meet me in the space where I am and not ask me stupid questions like how I am and say stupid things like how much he loves me.

Instead, I receive moments of extraordinary grace from strangers.

A woman I hardly spoke to in law school messages me to say that she lives near me and can walk my dog whenever I need.

My brother's friends send me hundreds of pictures and texts and videos I have never seen before and maybe this means my memories of him will never degrade, even though these aren't my memories and I wasn't there. His friends visit him at the rehab center every other weekend, even though it's an hour away from the city and it has now been months since the accident. I am touched that they don't fade away, even when his head is deflated and his eyes are blank and bloodshot and sometimes we have to send them to the waiting room while we reposition his catheter.

For my first case at the firm (seventy-eight municipalities about to become bankrupt), I am assigned to a Senior Associate. I am apprehensive because I have a vague memory of him from when I was a summer associate as a cordial but weary person. At the time, I didn't know if he was miserable or unfriendly. Mentor tells me that this will be a good assignment for me and that he will understand because he, too, has lost someone.

When I meet the Senior again, he is not the person I remember. He is friendly, if not warm. I tentatively explain my situation, and he has nothing but sincere empathy for me. He reassures me time and again that most people don't work all weekend anyway, that I have nothing to feel bad about, that I am fine.

"Remember, we just work here. Nothing here is that important. Nothing should take precedence over your family, especially while you're at the hospital. I want you to promise me that you will not work when something more important is happening."

Unprompted, he tells me about the night his mother passed away. How he was home taking care of her and then was forced to go into work for some forgotten reason. While he was out, his mother died.

I remember returning to my grandpa's body, waxen and yellow. I realize that the summer I met this Senior must have been only months after his mother's passing.

"In Judaism, you mourn for a year, and after that, you're supposed to affirmatively move on. In a sense, it's easier that way."

But I am in stasis. I cannot mourn one who is both living and dead. He stares at me with his same face and eyes, but everything is blank. This liminal space holds me prisoner. Show me the way, little crab.

"Maybe he'll get better. You never know."

Yeah, maybe.

(I do know. I knew the moment the nurse told me without hesitation to tell my parents to fly in from Korea. I knew the moment he opened his eyes and they were empty. I know we are clinging to a shade.)

The Senior calls me periodically to ask how I am. I tell him I am fine. He doesn't believe me and tells me to take care of myself, and I feel less alone in my grief.

Lil Chano from 79th

My brother used to send me the most indecipherable messages. "Listen to this song Cocoa Butter Kisses RIGHT NOW! Actually the whole mixtape. Prom Night. Hey Ma. Good Ass Intro. Chain Smoker. Acid Rain. He's my role model. I have friends who hang out with members of his crew. If I ever meet him, I will swoon. In a totally manly way that commands respect. Did you listen to Pusha Man? I know Nitty. I have his number in my phone. We share the same hookup!"

Four years later, when I finally understood what he was talking about, I asked my brother: "Have you ever heard of this song Cocoa Butter Kisses? It's really good. By this guy Chance the Rapper, you've probably never heard of him. He's from Chicago. Acid Rap is excellent, you should give it a try. He has a new album called Coloring Book, too. I bet you didn't know that."

I laughed as he screamed in mock frustration, and I made it a hobby to send him sporadic texts about new discoveries and memories that I stole from him. I would repeat back to him, word for word, things he had told me years back.

Like:

"Once, I was on this field trip, and I wanted to buy this little goat figurine, but I didn't have enough money, so my friend bought it for me."

"This is IDENTITY THEFT. Stop taking my memories!"

Now, at his bedside, I play Coloring Book for him over and over and over again. I place the speaker right next to his ear. I wonder if those neural correlates are still there, whether anything is flowing through that direct aural connection to the brain, the last thread to go. Sometimes, I even deign to play Drake or an old song my brother used to listen to in high school, in case he actually is in there but has gone back in time a bit. I tell him about my day and learning to be a lawyer and that B. and

I are engaged but haven't set a wedding date. I tell him the old bedtime stories of Eurydice and Orpheus, Persephone and Hades, Cerberus the many-headed hound, but without his interjections, my words trail off.

At random moments, I shout to evoke a startle response from him. At first, I believe he can hear me. Does he have neural correlates that map to my voice? Is his DNA more susceptible to my shouts than to others? He once told me that volume alone generally is not persuasive, but that somehow I could be both impossibly loud and commanding at once. I took this as a compliment and he said it was one, and now I think my voice might wake him up.

The doctors tell me to stop that, it isn't good for him. It is only matter. Automatic firing of action potentials without emergence of consciousness.

Hear me, brother. Would that my voice could electrify life into his brain.

∞. Time Travel

Sometimes I will remember something and, with a jolt, realize that it is from before the accident. The memory is so strong in my mind that I believe for a moment that, if I concentrate and tether myself to that memory strongly enough, I can bring myself back, through time, to save you.

8 Months, 10 Days. February (Entropy)

It is my father's birthday today.

After the first three months of emergencies, the surgeon puts steel plates into my brother's head, and he looks like himself again. Whole. We celebrate how good-looking he is, and we tell him that his head looks even better now than it did before the accident.

Then the right plate gets infected. They take the plate out and his head deflates. Then back in. Then back out. Then back in. Then back out. Re-curse-ive. We ask why there is a pinhole in his right side, but the doctor tells us it's a divot, not a hole.

"See, I can measure it. It's barely a millimeter. Not a hole."

My brother is stable today, so while my mother goes to check his vitals, I make a seed- and nut-encrusted black bass in a sweet and sour jus (my brother's favorite), slivers of roasted veal, and a chestnut and walnut loaf. I buy a bottle of champagne and my father's favorite red wine.

My mother comes back from the hospital and whispers to me that the pinhole has grown. We eat dinner, but eventually we have to tell my father.

Not a big deal, we say. That's what the doctor said.

But finally they tell us that the small divot that the doctor dismissed as a scab (even though we asked, again and again, why it was leaking, and we were told to calm down, to calm down, to calm down) is actually a hole boring into his skull. An infection is breaking down the skin already stretched taut around his head. It is a thin tarp, a drumskin in need of a patch. For the first time, I understand trypophobia.

The surgeon says:

"We can do another operation. Attack the site of the infection and, in four to six months, try to replace the plate again. Another option is to leave the plate out permanently and keep him in a helmet, which might lessen the chance of this infection recurring."

It takes work to keep everything ordered. To live is to fight entropy. You, for example, are a higher-level being, an ordered collection of molecules and cellular functions. It takes a lot of energy to keep you as you are. So when you die, your cells spread out. Entropy returns nature to a more balanced state.

"It is your choice. We are willing to do whatever procedure that you believe is best for him, and that we believe is a viable, medical option that we would be able to perform."

Less work, more balance. The natural state of things is to be balanced, for cells to be spread equally. It's elegant. Creates a level playing field. It's one of my favorite concepts.

"Another option is to make him comfortable. At this point, to be realistic, we don't know that he will get any better from here. Any procedure now would be to maintain his current state."

It is my father's birthday today.

February 28. Greenberg 14 South

High roller to the end. I guess all of those frequent-flier miles and hotel points that my brother racked up at his job did him good, because the nurses bring him to a suite on the top floor of the hospital with high ceilings and huge windows that overlook the East River, the same view my grandpa had when he died. I leave work in the middle of the day and hastily email all of my case teams that I am headed to the hospital.

The ward is not what I expect. The sheets are an expensive Italian brand and a robe in the bathroom tells me that the sheets and robes are for purchase if they are to our liking (price upon request). The lobby serves pineapple-infused water and high tea each afternoon. The pantry is fully stocked with beverages and individual serving cups of artisanal ice cream. Each morning, they bring us a menu for the day with "American" and "International" options.

One of my case teams say they are terribly sorry to bother me, but could I please answer some questions about a spreadsheet. I call them from the hospital lobby and, with admirable self-restraint or cowardice, I don't tell them to please go fuck themselves.

Mentor takes over. She tells each of my teams to stop emailing me immediately, and that I will be out of the office until further notice. She contacts the benefits department. She meets me at Frank E. Campbell to help me find an urn for my brother's ashes. I feel nothing until I walk into the coffin room and the soft-spoken undertaker explains the receptacle options that are compliant with the state law on cremation. I see a plain, pine box, and I imagine my brother shut up in this little cage before going up into flames, and I cannot breathe.

Thank you, I say. Mentor walks me back to the hospital and gives me some books to pass the time. My father tells me to buy an urn online. Mentor and the Senior and my officemate send the most beautiful white flowers to my brother's room, and my mother says she wants to recreate them in her flower arrangement class when she goes back home. We place the flowers on the windowsill and the petals float on an ultralight beam.

My parents watch Korean dramas during the day as we monitor my brother's breathing. My halmoni's caretaker in Seoul calls my mother with a crisis, which my mother solves calmly from my brother's bedside. With halmoni safe, the caretaker passes the phone to grandma, her voice small and shaky as she tries hard not to cry so she can be strong for us.

Sometimes, I wonder if I am the one who is dying. Did I succeed back then? Maybe I am in a coma, and the doctors are showing my mother and my father and my brother this sad reality I have created for myself. Maybe I am being punished. If I reach out in just the right way, can I part the veil? Will I see that this is all a dream?

We casually plan for after. Cremation. As soon as possible. No funeral, no wake, a small service with the family up at our house if we must.

My father tells me that when time comes for him, he doesn't want this. He wants to go quickly. But not too quickly, so he can enjoy the morphine before he goes.

My brother's breathing becomes calmer and quieter. The hospital agrees to withhold all food. My father asks outright whether they can give him a large dose of morphine. They gently tell us this isn't allowed in New York, but that they will keep him as comfortable as possible.

My mother says she knows she must let him go and in her voice I hear all of my fears—if this is right, if we are killing him, if inside his head he is screaming at us to bring him back, if inside his head he is screaming at us to let him go, if inside his head there is nothing because he left us long ago and we have been clinging to a vessel.

His friends ask to visit, and we let them in, one by one. They come in as grown men and hold his hand and tell stories and laugh with him, and they leave as small boys, sobbing because they miss their friend. Two of them share with me a picture of a napkin my brother left for them once, when he crashed on their couch after a night out:

Innkeeps—
Thank you for the food & lodging. I trust I will be back within the fort-night.
—M.

The women mostly keep it together until they leave. There are a lot of them—he was always surrounded by pretty women who were smarter than he was.

I send my parents home one evening so they can shower and sleep in a real bed. I drag a couch next to my brother's bed and I hold his puffy hand while we sleep. I wake up to the sunrise over the East River.

"Good morning. See how pretty it is outside! We had a sleepover like we used to."

(Sometimes, even when he was far too old for this, he would watch a scary movie and then ask me for a story and "accidentally" fall asleep in my bed, in case there were monsters.)

When my parents come back in the morning, we look through pictures of my brother. My father's favorite is the one of him laughing and petting Lilly, and I ask B. to go get it printed and framed.

As I am showing my parents the different frame options, I look over and I call out his name, but I know he has gone. Silence. His skin is sallow and a gray gloom has fallen over him. There was no change, but everything is different.

Why wasn't I next to him? What if he tried to cry out in that last moment and none of us heard?

My mother wails and holds him. My father gathers us together and tells us that my brother lived a full, happy life, and what we have left are the good memories we shared with him.

I get the doctor to declare the time of death. I handle the death certificate and the identification of the body and the release of the body to the crematorium, a process that involves an incompetent hospice director screaming at me and Mentor having to send me the statutory provision I can cite to prevent them from cutting into a body that has already suffered eight months of mortification.

(I never raise my voice, but after I receive the ashes, I destroy the hospice director's life.)

The morgue director calls me in the morning to confirm that I have a religious objection to a full autopsy. "Buddhist, right?" Sure, I say, even though I indicated nowhere in my written objection that I was Buddhist. I suppose with an Asian last name and yellow skin, I couldn't possibly fit into any of her other religious categories. I don't care, as long as this interminable process comes to an end.

I send B. a message to please straighten up the apartment so that it is neat for my parents. It seems important for some reason. We stop by an empty, spotless apartment to pick up Lilly and all of my liquor and my water bottle and we drive straight up to our house that night. In the car, my mother calls her mother and cries to her that he is gone. As I take a sip from my bottle, I realize that B. filled it with fresh ice cubes and cold, sweet water.

I am to break the news to the family. I email them that my brother went peacefully in his sleep and to please not contact us until we call them up for the memorial service.

At the house, my father opens a bottle of honey wine. "He never saw this house."

Days before the accident, we drove up to see this house on a lake that my father had wanted to buy for years. My mother and I pleaded with my brother to come with us, but he said he was busy, that he didn't feel like it, that he had plans. (Those plans included running to and from Brooklyn from the Upper West Side, and I never understood why. I assumed there was a girl involved.) So he never came, and instead, when we got back to the apartment, I showed him pictures of the house and we ordered dim sum and watched television.

All of the time and money my parents spent bringing him to violin lessons and piano lessons and baking baseball mitts and sending him to tutoring and Andover and college and buying him nice suits and cool sneakers and squash rackets for his tournaments and getting him internships and renovating our basement and ordering a special bed and wheelchair that my mother had to call to cancel because we won't be needing them anymore, thank you. Everything they poured into him, archived as a memory. Where does it all go?

I don't know how to become an only child.

My dad takes a drink. "I had a dream last night. There was a huge, gorgeous waterfall. Through the waterfall, I could see a house, a large, beautiful, comfortable house. I bought that house. But it was empty, and it was not for me. It was for M."

I sit next to my dad and take a sip of wine and tell him that I love him, something that I have never said to him without prompting. I feel in that moment, as I never have before, the intensity of his regret and fear and love for us, a scared dad muddling his way behind the frozen facade of a formal father.

I send a message to C., my best friend, the keeper of my brain, to tell everybody I know not to contact me under any circumstances. She keeps the wolves at bay, and I do not hear a word from anyone.

I sleep without dreaming.

Messier 83. Spiral Galaxy

The ashes are delivered to us on Saturday morning in a cardboard box. They are heavy, and small. I wonder if these are really his ashes, and how I would ever know, and whether it matters.

We place the ashes in the urn along with some photographs. Is this it? Is he trapped in this box? What am I talking to when I cry at the altar we create?

Family filters in for the service.

I am instructed to give a eulogy. I have nothing to say, except that he was better than me in every way, and everyone loved him more than they loved me, and rightfully so. That he wrote once that I was his heroine, only he spelled it heroin, but it was I who looked up to him for his patience and kindness and openness. That once, an older kid bullied him in elementary school and took his shiny Pokémon cards, so I found the bully and told him that this was unacceptable behavior, and the boy, terrified, offered to give back any cards I wanted. My brother was so excited to get his shiny cards back.

I can't remember any other reason he ever looked up to me.

My dad stands up. He shifts his weight back and forth on his feet and tells us that there isn't much to say.

My mother doesn't get up at all.

My mother's uncle tells us that when he first heard about the accident, he felt my brother's spirit leave in that moment, and knew he was gone. This was just his body.

We have nothing to say to that, but it seems to ease some of my mother's guilt.

When everyone leaves, I use my brother's remaining airline miles to book a flight to Reykjavik. I choose a cabin on Búrfellsvegur, which is to say, far enough from civilization to be in the middle of nowhere but close enough to a grocery store that I won't die if I don't want to. I want only to withdraw into a barren desert of ice where nothing grows.

I drive to all corners of the country, trying my best not to be blown off the road in the fierce, bone-chilling death winds, and I remember the last time I came to Iceland with K. and G. and C. I retrace the steps we took in Reykjavik as I listen to a radio play about Bohr and Heisenberg and the mysterious meeting they had in Copenhagen during the war. I am an unobserved particle, colliding into whatever crosses my path and letting the disruption guide me to my next point.

I go farther. Beyond the Golden Circle, to the next lagoon, to the next cliff, to the black sand beach at Vík, to the ice caves in the east, to a hidden waterfall in a shrouded glen, wherever my hand steers. I go dogsledding. I snorkel in the glacial water in the tectonic fissure at Þingvellir. I eat hákarl at a curious shark museum I accidentally discover while I am lost. I climb Helgafell and make three silent wishes. Maybe one of those wishes should have been to descend intact, because I might fall right off the ice and break my neck.

My GPS decides to be my tour guide. It takes me one way, and on the way back sends me another way, through Nesjavellir, through a snowy, winding mountain pass by a glassy lake and steaming hot spring. I am alone in the universe.

I start talking to my brother as if he is in the car with me, as if we are on one of our drives to Andover or playing a game in his room in Seoul. And then I am screaming and screaming and screaming and the Chasm in me widens still. I cannot reconcile what cannot be, and yet what is.

I leave a bottle of bourbon on a high shelf with a note for the next guests to have a drink in honor of M.

I fly into a blizzard, back to my parents' house, to be with the only people who can understand me in this moment.

TI-84. Where There's Not a Will
M., being of no mind and no body:

To me: His books, in the hope that I will better understand who he was. (I am sorry I didn't read *Cannery Row* until now. It was extraordinary. Is it you who wrote "Wow." in pencil in the margins under where Doc explains to Hazel why he thinks the stinkbugs are praying?)

His passwords, in the hope that I will find some inkling of his thoughts. (Don't worry, I deleted all of your risqué posts before umma looked through your phone, although a woman from your office came by with a box of your things while I was out, including Polaroids of a naked woman and the cigarillos I brought you from Puerto Rico. Umma was pretty speechless, which was a little funny. Why on earth did you keep those things in your office, of all places?)

His airline miles, which I use for my escape to Iceland. (Thanks, brother.)

My anguish that, even on the last night I saw him, I was only half paying attention to him as he talked about his future. (I was setting up my new watch. It seemed important at the time.)

The pen he stole from Jungsik after he bought me an extravagantly expensive dinner there. ("I just gave them $400, I can have a pen.")

The picture I took of him when we ate lunch at Bouley. He is looking up and rolling his eyes as if he is sooooo bored. He paid then, too, for both B. and me. ("It's your graduation present. You have to be my defense lawyers when you pass the bar.")

His retirement contributions (which he once told me about and warned me not to bump him off for the tiny sum that had accrued in his second month of work), to be rolled over into an inherited four-oh-wonk. (I take the lump sum instead, because I don't understand any of the other options and I have no future.)

Anything else of his that I want. (I take his Theory coat that I always borrowed without asking, and a few knickknacks that my mother wants to throw out.)

My hope that God is real and heaven is real and my brother knows how much I loved him and how sorry I am and how there was no one more fun, more infectiously lively, more loving, more innocent. Is this my will or his? These words are meaningless. They are the glimmers that die when you pluck a glowing leaf, the words you read in the obituary of every beloved son. They are just platitudes on a page if you didn't know him.

To no one: His TI-84 Plus, because the math genius always lost his things and had me buy him new ones.

To the Central Park Conservancy: $10,000 so I can sit on a bench with his name on it and pretend I am alive. (I have a year to think of an inscription and all I can think about are updog jokes and quotes from Calvin and Hobbes.)

To halmoni: No mention of his death. (It won't matter. I come home and she asks me every morning when he is going to visit. I tell him I miss him too, and that we will see him soon.)

To grandma: Not seeing him in his hospital bed, so her last memory of him is a whole, intact, laughing boy.

To grandpa: Maybe they will find each other. I don't know where my neural correlates for faith are.

To appa and umma: Everything else. The unbearable, unavoidable burden of choice—to let his body go in the peace and dignity it had left, into the natural state of balanced entropy.

85. ἄστατος

His friends tell me this is what he would have wanted. He would have wanted to go without being a burden. He would have wanted most of all for our parents to be happy.

I don't think he would have wanted to go at all.

I dream him, and I remember him, and sometimes I don't remember which is which.

My mother used to oil and bake baseball mitts in the oven for him when we lived in New Jersey. We tried so hard to be American, and we were happy.

I dream that B. and I are driving in Yosemite and my brother is in the back seat. We decide to go to Tuolumne Meadows because the main park is so crowded. My brother says he wants to go motor-biking or dirt-biking crossed with hoverboarding. I tell him he can try that tomorrow if he is careful and wears a helmet.

I dream I am holding a baby swaddled in white. People are being irresponsible with her. I keep trying to cuddle her and stop her from crying. I try to feed her, but she won't latch and I have no milk so I give her a bottle. I have to perform CPR multiple times, once with my elbow. It doesn't work and the baby dies, but then she comes back.

I dream I am in a battlefield to stop a giant from preying on a baby, and also to protect my brother, who is paralyzed. Then he comes in, standing, able to walk, and we are stunned. I hug him tightly and so do my parents. We explain that we were waiting, that they told us he would never get up, never walk. We tell him how much we love him.

I remember my brother, a little boy, running around in our yard and pausing and sticking out his butt to pretend he is a firefly. And then a few years later, waking me up at the crack of dawn to walk him to the town pond so he could learn how to fish. We realized only later that fish did not live in that pond.

I dream that my brother is going to get another surgery, but then I make a funny face at him and he begins to smile and laugh and respond.

I dream that my halmoni has already died twice and she is standing upright and knows who I am, and we say our goodbyes because she knows she will die at 9:38. She lies down and dies and it is 9:37. I scream twice in despair.

I remember my brother trying to answer a question in a trivia game about adages. "The road to hell is paved with . . . ice cubes? No, wait, that's heaven, because hell would be hot . . ."

I remember him learning about Ralph Waldo Emerson one summer, and thereafter responding to any request for a cup of water or to pass the salt or to do the dishes by shaking his head no, his eyes closed, nose turned up, saying, "Self-Reliance, by Ralph Waldo Emerson" before dissolving into laughter.

I remember us watching a movie in which a thief has to sneak by a tangle of red lasers. We recreated the laser maze in my room out of red yarn and bells. We devised an elaborate way of snaking through the strings until my dad told us to clean up the mess. Later, when we moved to Korea, we created traps in each other's rooms, bells to warn us of intruders, contact plates with tin foil and batteries in the floor.

I dream that my brother is up and about. In my dream, I fear I am dreaming so I ask everyone else if they can see him, and they say they can. I can't believe my good luck. And then I wake up for real.

I dream he was electrocuted but slowly begins to come back one word at a time. I am in a pool and I swim back and forth, telling him how much I missed him.

I dream my brother is in New York and beginning to wake up. He has moments of lucidity and then slumps over, gone again. But his lucid periods grow longer and longer, and when he is awake, he is normal, funny, watching television with earphones. I ask what he could hear while he was sleeping, and he said he could hear his friend. I call my dad because I am so afraid my brother will relapse and we will miss our window somehow. Then in my dream, I wake up and worry that this was all a dream. But it is real. But then I wake up again and I am truly awake this time.

In my dream, it is time. People come in from all over to say goodbye, and it isn't even his memorial yet. His friends fill Central Park. They spread down the coast and create an unbroken line of torches. His friends from Andover insist on bringing back the ruins of a raft they had, and I can see my brother's happy face, laughing. I am so happy to see so many people here for my brother. My dad drives to the front of the line in a car through the Central Park loop and everyone sees us. They pay us their respects.

I dream I am flying back and forth between New York and Iceland, and I am angry about working. My brother is in and out of my dream, but his death is present. I check his ashes as I bring him up to a ziggurat to be buried. In the end, I am hugging my brother and telling him he can never die.

In my dream, I know I am dreaming, and I want to see you. And then suddenly there you are, up in a tree, but your face is so dry, the way it sometimes was at the hospital. I want to hug you, to kiss you, but you turn away and won't speak to me. I wish for you to be happy, and I tell you how much I love you.

I dream we are painting my room. He is helping me paint, but mostly being mischievous. It is Christmas, and we can't decide what to get anyone. We hide under our old dining table and ask each other what we got. We are younger. In this dream, I don't know that he has died.

I dream that my brother and his friend come to me and tell me there is a huge problem and that they need to talk to me in secret. My brother tells me, "I used my credit card . . ." I'm not sure what this has to do with anything, and then I realize that if he used his credit card, it means he isn't dead, that he was faking it all along, even though I saw his body at the hospital. I wonder how my first thought upon seeing him wasn't shock. I tell him this is fixable, and we can just claim credit card fraud.

I dream we are pulling the plug on my brother but it is a mistake because he spoke, he said it hurt, and I knew he could maybe get better, but the doctors say this was only one sentence and it is too late to change our minds. But he spoke. He was getting better.

I dream we are in a speakeasy café in Korea. I am mad at my brother for some reason, but he is trying to gloss over it. We are discussing whether we want to buy the special edition Calvin and Hobbes books from the café.

I dream that I hold a toddler in a bright red parka and I know it is my brother. He is so small and snuggly.

I have a dream that I have no dreams. That I have nothing else to work for, and I might as well die.

I can't decide whether it is worse to dream or not to dream.

If I could live in K.'s machine, if he could recreate M. for me, if his abomination of neuroscience could take me back and feed me a simulation of my family, unbroken, I would leap at the chance.

Would it matter to me that my brother would still be dead, if I didn't know? Would a wraith of him suffice to bring me out of this Chasm? Do I want him back for his own good or for mine?

Would he want to come back?

Eighty-Sixed

My grief has frozen me in time, but my law firm still expects me to bill in six-minute increments.

"We don't have a billable hours target."

(But they do look at your hours to see if maybe you need more work.)

"We are committed to a diverse firm and partnership."

(The photographs of the annual partnership election announcements speak for themselves.)

"We don't differentiate between paying and pro bono hours."

(This is a lie.)

The Senior does his best to ease me back in gently, but there is only so much he can do. He tells me, bluntly, that all of this is going to be terrible and unbearable for a long time, and I appreciate that I am not being fed an insipid line about how it will be better soon and that my brother is in a better place. I work harder than I did before I left, so many billable hours, and I push everything else into the back of my mind until it bursts out at the most inopportune moments (the grocery store; on the phone with customer service; explaining to a paralegal that numerical order means 1 comes before 10).

I do my work. I try to do it well. I have a pressing need to be useful, although I'm not sure why or to whom. I catch myself trying to calculate what time I started writing a text, or loading the dishwasher, and then I remember that normal, non-psychotic, non-lawyers do not, in fact, measure their lives in 0.1-unit, six-minute increments.

I wonder how much I would have billed if I had tracked the time I spent by his bedside.

I don't know how to reconcile the guilt of my prolonged absence from work with my inability to function. And again, I wonder if my trauma and my family are a crutch, an excuse for each time I send something out that I know isn't the best it could be.

And then I remember that I don't care because nothing matters.

Messier 87. Supermassive Black Hole.

Days after my brother is reduced to ashes, B. asks me about putting down a wedding deposit.

Not now.

"Do you want to talk about it?"

Not now.

"But are you holding off because you don't want to at all?"

I don't bother answering. But then my parents offer to pay the wedding deposit, and I can't tell them no. They tell me they want me to be happy, to look forward and not look back, and if this is the person I want to marry, they are happy to help.

B. and I walk home from work and begin to plan the wedding in earnest.

Then:

"I didn't want my parents to think they needed to contribute, because they don't have a lot of money."

That's fine. This is a gift from my parents to us.

"I told them your parents generously offered to use some of M.'s life insurance proceeds for the money, so that my parents wouldn't feel like they have to contribute."

Excuse me?

"It was just so that my parents wouldn't feel awkward. Are you mad?"

Go home. I do not want to see you. Do not contact me.

He bikes off, and he doesn't understand what he's done. Maybe he has done nothing, maybe I am overreacting, what does it matter the white lies we tell? It's just money. It's meaningless.

Money I never wanted. Money I shouldn't have. Money from an accident that split open my brother's skull and extinguished a future of laughing and eating sriracha and playing squash and tricking people into asking what updog is.

B. comes back to my apartment two days later. He starts to explain himself, and I scream at him with a more destructive rage than I ever knew I had. μῆνιν ἄειδε θεὰ so I can stop screaming. I have never screamed at another human before, even when that incompetent hospice director was screaming at me as I watched my brother's body cool. But now I am a black hole of wrath.

I tell my mother I hate him, and she tells me to forgive him. He doesn't understand. He will learn. You have a long life ahead of you. Remember he loves you.

My dad flies back to Korea to go back to work. He wants nothing more than to move forward and not look back. My mother tells him that she needs more time here so that I won't be alone. He reluctantly agrees, and she stays at the house, alone, in the room where we placed the ashes and the picture of my brother petting Lilly, and his favorite stuffed Hobbes doll I got for him years ago. I tell her I don't need to go back to work, that I can stay with her, but she doesn't want me there. For three weeks in her thirty years of marriage, she is unobserved, undisturbed, existing in all states at once.

K.'s wedding is in a week. I tell my mother I can skip it, but she tells me to go.

I fly to California alone, and I congratulate K. and his parents and his new wife. I leave early before my bitterness begins to surface. K. catches me as I am slipping out of the door and even though he is drunk and high on the ecstasy of his moment, he holds me close and tells me he knows it was hard for me to come, and he so wanted me to be there, and thank you for coming.

My mother is packing when I get back. She says she has run out of excuses to be alone, although I tell her that she owes nothing to anyone, and that if there is a time for any of us to be selfish, this is it. She tells me I will understand when I get married, that it is time to return to her life and to my halmoni, and she flies home to trade one patient for another.

88. Constellations

His utter failure—arrogance, cowardice, anguish, valor, as you will—was rewarded with heavenly immortality. A lyre, crowned by Vega, the messenger of light, the falling eagle, the conqueror. A divine instrument emerging from scattered points of light in the night sky. (Or, if you prefer, 織女, Weaver Girl, permitted to join her family once a year on the seventh day of the seventh month.)

Moved by his love, the gods transformed Orpheus into a swan and reunited him with his lyre, ever shining through the darkness. Or was this a punishment? Written in the heavens in fire and ice, the farthest he could possibly be from his lost love?

I write the lyre on my skin. Not for him, that fool, but for my family:

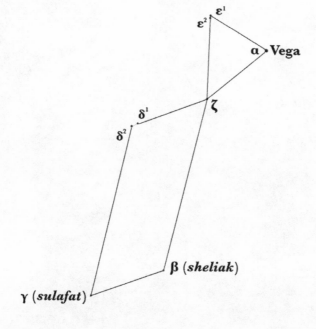

α Lyrae, Vega, the light that left the star when I was born.

ε^1 and ε^2 Lyrae, double-double, my mother and father.

ζ Lyrae, our center, my father's mother.

δ^1 and δ^2 Lyrae, optical double, my mother's mother and my mother's father.

β Lyrae, *sheliak*, explosion of eclipsing stars, my brother.

γ Lyrae, *sulafat*, yoked to my brother, Lilly, who sometimes still noses into his room wondering where her 멍멍이 companion has gone.

1989–???

My life is refuse scattered across time. I cannot point to a single moment that would prevent me from jumping at the chance to rewind to before the accident, to before my grandpa, to before I spat in my halmoni's face by rejecting her beautiful clothes, to before that night or that other night, to before anything I have ever lived. I find nothing worth preserving.

Why did Lot's wife look back?

Did she have a name?

90. In Ruth Bader Ginseng's name we pray, a(wo)men.

A month before my halmoni turned ninety, when I was still in law school, my brother and I decided to fly to Seoul for Christmas. Alone, Korea is a hazy, foreign country. With my brother, who spoke less Korean than I do, it was a home.

He arrives at the business class lounge in sunglasses, with twenty foil-topped packets of water in tow. "I went out last night."

"But why don't you get a big bottle of water?"

"Because they only have water for ants. These need to be at least three times bigger." He drinks each tiny bottle and creates a pyramid.

He is almost recovered by the time we board, and he insists that we watch every episode of Top Chef that I have on my computer. I doze off somewhere in the middle of season four, and he shakes me awake asking if I know how to cook this and that. Sure, I mumble, we can make all of that when we get home, once I finish writing my paper.

We run out of Top Chef episodes by the time we land, so I turn on Top Chef Masters for him as I try to write the note I need to finish for my law degree. I leave my computer for a moment, and I return to a new paragraph:

And by the power invested in the shareholders of the united arab jemerates, and henceforth witherto albeit hereafter habeas corpus ex post factos.[9] In Ruth Bader Ginseng's name we pray, a(wo)men. Thank you and good night.

[9] JUDGE JUDY.

I give up on the paper. While he is out grocery shopping, he texts me that the store has nothing I requested.

"TOM CARPACCIO[1] HAS THROWN A TWIST. You must adapt.
Thank goodness for my swift marshon-plooje[2] to prep the 'gredients."

We make do, somehow, as I cook and he throws diced apples at me,
and we serve a seven-course dinner: a platter of salty green olives and
juicy figs stuffed with soft, ripe cheese; a delicate, gold-rimmed china
tureen of spiced squash soup swirling with ribbons of rich cream and
dotted with twinkling pomegranate seeds; a steaming pot of black mus-
sels in garlic; bowls of roasted, glazed eels over sticky white rice; ladles
of savory oxtail stew; spoonfuls of silky egg custard; clusters of plump
black grapes and syrup over crunchy shaved ice. Even my halmoni, who
doesn't know it's Christmas, eats some of the squash soup we give her
and takes a sip of plum wine.

A week later, on New Year's Day, my brother and I bow to her, and she
kisses us each on the cheek.

"Happy New Year." She says this in English.

Next, we bow to grandma, who cries a little, and our parents, who give
us envelopes with more money than adult children need.

We eat rice cake soup, and my brother and I make plans to go to each
of the Michelin-starred restaurants when we get back to New York.

("Maybe we shouldn't have given you two all of that money . . .")

My halmoni stops eating the next day and will only open up if my
dad sings and dances and flies the spoon into her mouth. I don't know
if she has forgotten how to swallow or simply refuses, so we feed her one
spoonful of porridge at a time and play the airplane game, singing children's songs as if she is a toddler. I wonder if, deep inside whatever is left
of her brain, my halmoni despises us for keeping her here.

1 Tom Colicchio.
2 Mise-en-place.

91 Wedding Guests

In the end, I let B. come back.

I loved him once. I wanted to marry him once. I tell myself it would be imprudent to make an impulsive, life-altering decision when I am in a haze of grief that crowds out any other feeling. The most rational path forward is to make the decision I would have made, had I not lost everything.

Or maybe I am sitting on a train that has already left the station, and it is too much effort to jump off.

I tell B. he is in charge of planning the wedding. I will pick the music and show up in a dress. My wedding march will be a Nina Simone song.

B. creates a wedding website, and we send out save-the-date cards to ninety-one guests. The cards show a picture of us from when we were in Puerto Rico at G.'s wedding, before all of this happened. We are on the beach and I am mid-laughter, because the photograph is actually a still from a video that an old man took for us because he didn't know how to use my camera.

We went swimming in the ocean right after this. The sea looked calm, but a riptide dragged me under into a dark, burning chaos—

—waves collapsing over my head, obscuring my vision and tossing me in every direction

—seawater pouring down my throat and nostrils, pushing me back under the surface each time I manage to find air

—panic increasing as I struggle toward light and air and sky

—the sparkling, salty, wine-dark sea screaming into my lungs and streaming into my eyes as I sputter and choke and flounder and founder

Is this how I die? I'm not—

Then B. grabs my arm and steadily, miraculously, pulls us both out of the vortex and back to shore. I cling to him, gagging and speechless and stunned at how much I wanted to live, but didn't know how to wrench myself out of the devouring whirlpool.

In the photos, there is nothing of this. Just laughter and sand and sun. Our wedding website includes more pictures of us across the years, in Copenhagen, in Galway, in Almaty, in Portland. I think I must have been happy once, and I wonder why I can't remember.

For Thanksgiving, he brings me a puppy from St. Croix who barked her way out of a hurricane. The vet tells us she was born on June 11, the day of the accident, and I think maybe this is a sign. We put her in my brother's room so she can make friends with the ghost.

We name her Nova. Emergence of brilliance from a dying star. Or one who chases butterflies. Or one who doesn't walk, *no va*, because sometimes she will sit in the middle of the sidewalk and refuse to move until she is bribed with a piece of salmon.

My dad names her 말순이.

"What does that mean?"

"It means the last girl. This is what parents name their daughter when they want a son."

Lilly resigns herself to the fact that Nova, who is a quarter of her size, will always steal her toys.

I begin shopping for wedding dresses.

92. Merry-Go-Round

Every day, I forget my brother is dead. Every day, this memory hits me with the same savage force.

When my family mentions my brother, it is only in passing. When I mention him, it is as if he is still alive. I know what I am doing, and I don't correct myself. I haven't decided what I will say when I meet new people and they run out of interesting things to say and begin asking me if I have any siblings.

(The next time I go to the hairdresser in Seoul, she asks me if M. flew home with me to visit. I realize why my mother doesn't come to this hairdresser anymore.

No, I say. He didn't come with me.)

When my mother mentions him, she cries. "Stupid boy," she says, and I know that she and I will forever be together at his bedside, waiting for him to wake up.

B. breaks his back climbing, and I have my cousin drive me three hours up to a hospital in Poughkeepsie where they don't turn the MRI machine on during the weekends. For four sleepless nights in a freezing ICU room, I listen to the IV drip and the vitals monitor and measure his urine and smell the caustic cleaning chemicals of my brother's bedside and email the firm that I have had another family emergency and will not be in the office for a few days. B. has brought me back into my worst nightmare, the nightmare from which I cannot wake.

I am furious at having to play caretaker for this fool who doesn't deserve it, who brought this gratuitous injury upon himself, who will recover without a scar while my brother is black powder in a walnut urn. I tell B. I will not be my mother, I won't spend my life caring for other people and putting my life on hold, and the next time he decides to put his life on the line without thinking about who will be cleaning up his mess, I will not show up at the hospital. He tells me in a drug-induced fog how much he loves me and how he will always be there for me if anything happens to me.

Except something did happen to me, and he wasn't there.

I tell my mother and she, too, is furious. "Put in your prenup that he is banned from climbing outdoors."

"I don't think that's what prenups are for. But I'll look into it. He never reads anything he signs."

"Be nice to him now, though. While he's in pain."

"I'm coming home for Christmas. I'm sick of being here. I haven't seen halmoni in two years, and she is going to be ninety-two. Put up the Christmas tree!"

"We gave the tree away a long time ago, dummy. I'll find your Christmas merry-go-round, though." Pause. "So you are really going to come home for Christmas?"

"Yes, why? I want to see halmoni and I thought we could go to Jeju for a couple days."

"How early do you think you can come?"

"Why?"

"Halmoni has not been eating for a couple of days. We don't know if she forgot to swallow again or just doesn't want to but she hasn't swallowed any food or water this week. We are keeping her on an IV now, but there is only so much we can do, and your dad doesn't want to prolong this. Maybe it would be different if she were alert and healthy, but . . ."

"How long."

"It's not an emergency, it's more like now that she is on the IV, there is only so long she can hold out if she doesn't eat anything. We are sort of in control. Like with M."

"How long. My flight is in a few weeks. Is that too late?"

Pause.

"If your plan was to come over Christmas to see her, then maybe you should come now. But it is your choice. She doesn't recognize anyone, and we aren't going to make a big deal out of it. When the time comes, we will do it quietly, like with M. Nobody will be upset if you don't come, we will understand."

"I am coming tomorrow."

"I know you want to see her, but I don't know if I want you to sit by her and go through all of this again."

"I am coming tomorrow."

"Of course, this happened two years ago, and we called the aunts and everything, and all of a sudden she got better, so maybe the aunts will think I am the one who cried wolf. But I think it is different this time. I should have let her go a long time ago. I was selfish. But if I can let M. go, I can let her go."

"I am coming tomorrow. See you soon."

I tell the firm that I will be flying to Seoul for *yet another family emergency* and wonder if they will fire me now. How many emergencies can a person have in one year? I remind myself that the best approach is to emulate confidence, and also that no one ever really gets fired from a law firm.

I remember how closely Death walks with me every day and how little time I have left, and I can't believe I have wasted that time writing emails or worrying about work or watching television to fall asleep.

I give B. hasty instructions for the dogs and the apartment, and I head to the airport with a backpack. As I am putting my passport away on the plane, I find a letter tucked away in the front pocket.

> *I know the upcoming weeks (and later) are not going to be easy for you or your family, but please know through it all that, while I may not always understand the full extent of your thoughts or your feelings, I am always going to be there to listen, quietly, sometimes probably giving you so much space that it appears that I'm insensitive or aloof. But please take solace through it all that I've got a lifetime to be there for you, so if I don't get it quite right the first time, I will learn.*
>
> *Even under these circumstances, I hope that you're able to at least appreciate this time you do get to spend with your family. Please do not be stressed about taking this time off from work—everyone knows and appreciates your legal brilliance and hard work, as well as the circum-*

stances behind your absence. I'll do my best to take care of the dogs in
your absence, and not steal their affection too much.
   I cannot wait for you to return. My fondest regards.
   Yours,
   B.

"My fondest regards? What is this, 1811? You can say you love me."

"Wow. So mean."

"Putting my phone away now. Hope my plane doesn't get shot down by North Korea. Bye!"

I am in the same seat I sat in years ago with my brother. I remember, almost a decade ago, flying home with him during a school break and spending eight hours making him teach me how to solve a Rubik's Cube until I could do it perfectly.

I have always had a vague fear of flying, but this time I really think my plane might get shot down because relations with the North are more unstable than I remember in years. I wonder if I will feel anything. I make a note to confirm that the subway station in front of our apartment is a bomb shelter. (It is.)

I wake up at Incheon Airport intact. When I arrive home, my mother is in the middle of feeding my halmoni a full bowl of porridge.

"This was all a ploy!"

My mother swears this is the first time she has eaten in seven days.

I give my halmoni my brightest smile. "I missed you! I came from New York to see you."

"You did? From New York?"

"Yes, from New York. I missed you."

"You should have come from the beginning."

She hasn't been this responsive, my mother says. She is alert today.

"I know, I should have. Did you miss me?"

"Of course I missed you."

"Who am I?"

She is thinking.

"Who am I?"

"My granddaughter, of course. Is M. here? When is M. coming? I miss M."

I want to be where she is. Her eternal sunshine. "M. couldn't come but he says he misses you." I hand her a soft white teddy bear sitting on the kitchen counter.

"Your dad brought it for her from London," grandma says, watching my halmoni. "He gave us both one."

"Isn't this bear pretty?" I ask my halmoni.

"Yes, it is very pretty." My halmoni gathers it into her arms and examines its fuzzy head and green satin ribbon.

"Where did you get it?"

"I bought it."

"Can I have it?"

She frowns and shakes her head and tugs it close to her heart.

I am technically working remotely, which means I hold my halmoni's hand and research questions about indemnities while New York is sleeping, and draft deposition outlines while Seoul is sleeping. The emails I receive are cautious, tentative, wondering how I am doing, silently asking if she is dead yet, and I feel like a fraud because she ate an entire bag of chips and another bowl of porridge.

But then she stops eating again. My mother tries to trick her into swallowing her porridge by having her sing:

O my darling, o my darling, o my darling Cle-men-tine . . .

It doesn't work. We let her spit the food out, and then she sings along with us.

Talk to her, grandma says. See if she still knows who you are.

In English:

"Grandmother! How are you!"

"Fine."

"What is your name?"

"Ok Sun Hong."

"Where do you live?"

She just looks at me. She has exhausted the emergency responses we taught her when we lived in New Jersey.

I smile at her, and she smiles back.

"Do you know who I am? Who am I?"

"옥담이, my beloved sister, of course. Why didn't you come earlier? I missed you. You should have come earlier."

Yes, I tell her. It's me, your sister. I've come to eat breakfast with you, let's eat. I give her a piece of clementine, and she eats it.

And thereafter, every time I ask, she says I am 옥담이. I wonder if she was pretty.

"옥담이, my beloved sister, here you are . . ."

But then she looks at me curiously, and something in her knows that this is not right, that 옥담이 isn't here but in a North Korean grave, and she doesn't know this strange face staring at her.

Her trajectory is unplottable. She will ask for my dad in the morning and think he is her husband when he comes back from work in the evening. She will eat a full bowl of porridge for breakfast, and then refuse to drink even honey water for the next week. My mother connects her to an IV of essential nutrients (who needs a nurse when you spent a year watching your son die?) and I watch the milky white droplets that keep the entropy at bay for now.

Every day, I think today is the last day. I panic each time I look away from her and look back. I worry she has stopped breathing, that her gaze has turned to stone. But then she looks at me, and she is back.

"I'm getting married," I tell her.

"You're getting married?"

"Yes. Next year."

"When?"

"In the fall. Will you come to my wedding?"

"Of course I'm going to come to your wedding."

"What will you wear?"

"Of course I will wear a 한복."

"And what should I wear? A white dress or a 한복?"

"Of course you must wear a 한복. A beautiful one. Red."

And then it is Christmas Eve, somehow, and my mother finds my merry-go-round and plugs it in. The miniature carousel spins slowly as a medley of carols hums from its crackling speakers, and miniature figurines pop in and out of the carousel roof—a nutcracker drumming, an elephant twirling—as the carousel spins on and on. I remember Paris and cotton candy, and I don't mention this to my mother.

"It is Christmas, halmoni."

"Christmas? Already?"

My dad spends the day in her room playing carols for her and kissing her cheek. "This is probably my last Christmas with her."

He pulls out a mat and pillow to sleep next to her that night, the first time I have ever seen him sleep away from my mother in our house.

Christmas Day is bright but hazy. I can't see beyond the neighboring building, and my dad tells me to make sure all of the windows are shut tight to keep the smog and yellow dust out. "When she passes away, I will move out of this country. Can't even breathe here. I'm going to go back upstate to New York and get a German shepherd."

93. 홍
자
범

My dad comes into my halmoni's room with a box wrapped in clean white cloth. He places the box in her hands. "This is your husband. My father. These are his ashes."

She looks down at the box, which has her husband's name written on it vertically, in the old style.

"Read this. What does it say?"

She starts playing with the knotted silk.

"Your husband's ashes. These are his ashes. What does this say? Can you read this?"

She looks up at my dad.

"Do you know what this is? What is this? Read what it says."

She looks down again at the box, curiously, blankly. She says nothing.

"His ashes. These are his ashes."

My mother takes the box from him and wraps it in a bolt of patterned silk that is dark blue on one side and gray on the other. My dad leaves the room.

My mother carefully folds another bolt of the same cloth that she hasn't used.

"Is that for halmoni?"

"No, no, just an extra. I didn't know what size the box would be."

But ashes all come in the same size box, we know this. I wonder if my halmoni will see ninety-three. My mother points out that she is already ninety-three by Korean calculations, since we count the nine months before birth as a year.

I touch the bolt of silk and wonder how long it will be until I hold death in my hands again.

94. Plutonium

Over half a century after my halmoni's escape from North Korea, we continue to live in the shadow of partition.

"The ICBM technology isn't there yet. New York is probably fine."

"They are likely exaggerating their bomb test results."

"They may, however, have more plutonium than suspected."

My coworkers in New York talk about buying iodine pills and reserving a place in a fallout shelter. Mostly, though, it's arch, witty fodder for cocktail party conversations about the state of the world.

They don't live thirty miles from the DMZ and whatever lies beyond. By the time anyone has decided to strike, we will already be afterimages. I map out every bomb shelter within walking distance of our house, and I daydream about how I would carry my halmoni on my back, down into the earth.

Of course, if they decide to deploy chemical weapons instead, going underground might be useless. Maybe we would need to head as high as possible, to the mountains, gasping for clean air. I think of pious Aeneas carrying his father on his back out of Troy. I think of another story of another son who, on the order of the king, carried his mother on his back into the forest to die. He asked her as he walked why she kept snapping off twigs.

"So that you can find your way back home, my son."

He couldn't leave her, so he brought her back.

I don't remember how the story goes after that.

During some sleepless rabbit hole, I read an old article that tells me that the satellites we have already shot into space will remain circling the earth around us forever, undisturbed by earthly chemical destruction or nuclear winter or whatever fresh hell we create for ourselves.

I wonder if all of my emails and texts will survive on those satellites.

If someone will read everything I wrote to my brother, or decipher the troves of nonsense messages we sent to each other, or watch the footage of him flying through the air, or listen to his curated playlists. Whether whatever I leave will be enough for someone to fill in the gaps. What my life will look like through the lens of a stranger's interpolation.

I-95. New York to Boston

My brother and I once drove up to Boston from New York. It was St. Patrick's Day. I was going to visit C., and he wanted to visit some of his friends.

I liked driving with him because it was one of the few times we would talk without one of us distracted by work or television or texts. He told me he wasn't sure he believed in God the way we were raised, but that he had been exploring Buddhism lately. (Maybe the morgue director was right by accident, even though she was definitely a little racist.) I don't remember now what else we talked about—probably school, maybe girls—but I remember regretting that we were going to the same city to hang out with different people. I imagined, young as he was, that whenever he got married, he would have less and less time for me.

The January before the accident, I sent B. an email of my New Year's resolutions. Resolution 8: "Be more patient with M. Don't be afraid to have a serious chat with him about his life, because he probably needs it. Spend more time with him."

I definitely kept that last part. He just wasn't awake for it.

96th Street

What if we had moved into that apartment on 96th Street, instead? Would he be with me now in Korea, trying to get halmoni to eat, or would he have been thrown into the air twenty blocks north of where he was?

What if I had been more serious about telling him that he didn't need to go out partying every single weekend, instead of making fun of his weekly hangovers and telling him to grow up?

What if I hadn't gotten so caught up in my first years of dating B. and had spent more time with my brother when he first moved in with me?

What if I had convinced my brother to come to Marea with me that Saturday like we had planned? I had promised to buy him a fancy lunch as part of our Michelin tour. Instead, he told me that we should order in from Andy's Deli and relax because he was going out on Friday night, and it was going to be a hassle to get up on Saturday morning. (Andy's Deli was his favorite place because the food was good, cheap, and always came in fifteen minutes, unlike Andy's Deli II, which he said must be so named because they took twice as along. We once ended up ordering all three meals from the original Andy's Deli because every time we looked through the options that day, he said "... or maybe Andy's Deli?")

He had just come home from a business trip and was excited about his next project and what he planned to do. I had gotten a new watch and was setting it up while I was listening to him.

"Why aren't you listening to me while I'm telling you about my future!"

"I am, I am!" I repeated to him verbatim what he had just said.

"No fair to use your perfect short-term memory recall to pretend you're listening."

We walked out of the apartment that night together. We split off at

75th Street. I was going to walk to the train, and he was going to take a cab, because of course he was.

"Bye!"

"Don't lose your key!"

I knew he wouldn't be back by the time I got home, but when I woke up around three in the morning to go to the bathroom, I was surprised he wasn't back. I thought maybe I should call him, but decided he was probably having a big night and would ignore my call anyway.

I don't know if I would have been too late. I could check the file I have for the timestamp of the 911 call that the taxi driver made, but why? To read again and again six sentences, not about his life, but about how he is likely to die?

I remember again how my dad wanted to sue the taxi driver. I told him there were no grounds. The car was going twenty miles per hour. My brother stepped out into the middle of the street when the car had the light. The driver tried to swerve. He immediately stopped, got out of the car, and called 911. He didn't flee the scene, not like so many other hit-and-runs that have apparently occurred in that same area, which we only learned later, because who spends their time thinking about car accidents that will never happen to them? There was no evidence that the driver was texting or calling at the time of the collision. If he was momentarily distracted or dozed off, we would never know. And even so, would that be a basis for punishment? Who would that serve?

Later, when I am having coffee with my brother's best friend, this friend assures me that M. would never have done this on purpose, that I shouldn't even think that. And I think to myself that this wasn't even a thought I had until he put it into my mind.

The file I have contains the driver's name and phone number. I wonder once in a while whether I should call him, whether he would speak to me. Whether he wonders what happened to the boy he hit. Whether he thinks it's his fault, or knows it isn't. Whether he thinks about it at all.

I peek at the file and see his name.

Nematollah. God's blessing.

I close the file and delete it.

1997. First Woman President

After the first woman in United States history takes office as Secretary of State, I remember my halmoni telling me that I should become president when I grow up. She calls me into the kitchen one evening as she is making fishcakes for my brother and me.

"Promise me that you will be the first woman president. Do you promise?" She holds out her pinky.

I don't know what else to do, so I pinky swear with her. "I promise."

My mother has never let me live down the fact that I made a promise I obviously can't keep, because according to her, politicians need tact and I have none. She is not wrong.

If this were a different story, and if I were a different person, this might be the inspirational, motivational story of how, as my last gift to my dying halmoni, I overcame adversity and kept my promise after all those years to become the first woman president.

This is not that story, and I am not that person.

It takes all of my effort each day to make my will into reality.

It takes all of my effort each day not to make my Will into reality.

9.8 m/s²

I am afraid of falling and afraid of heights, so naturally I took up climbing as a hobby to make B. happy. It's a choice I quickly undid after I fell on a top-out route and tore all the tendons in my right arm, and after we went aid-climbing in Utah and a carabiner broke and I watched it fall thirty feet to the ground, and after my brother smashed his head and I realized I could not leave my parents with no children.

I fear one day B. will leave me for a woman who isn't afraid of falling or afraid of heights and who isn't (de)motivated by an ever-present fear of death. She will be graceful and beautiful and an excellent, fearless climber who can co-lead a big wall with him.

He thinks this is an irrational fear, but he doesn't deny that my refusal to climb is a disappointment. "It's my favorite thing to do, and it means we have less time that we can spend together."

"You don't have to go climbing every single weekend. We can do other things together that don't involve me falling to my death or accidentally dropping you to yours."

He agrees with this in theory, but reserves a rental car for a climbing trip every weekend, anyway. He is singularly focused on his goals, which is both admirable and incredibly annoying.

He is devoted to me. He doesn't understand me on an existential level, but he offers his love for me in tangible ways—woodworking, taking care of the dogs, doing the laundry, learning the Korean alphabet, bolting upright out of a sound sleep that time I started screaming at four in the morning because I found cockroach eggs in the corner of our closet, and immediately, unflinchingly, laughingly eradicating the entire infestation while I ran back under the covers and whimpered. He has never said no to anything I have directly asked of him, and, with the exception of trying to exorcise my acrophobia, accepts me entirely.

But each time he packs his climbing gear, I wonder if I will get another call, if I will have to explain that I really do have another family emergency in the form of a man who believes himself invincible. And I wonder how it is fair that he can so casually risk his body every week, but I must sanitize my answers every time he asks me how I am.

"I didn't kill myself today" isn't an answer he will understand, even though I probably don't really want to kill myself, and that's not what it means. But I can't find the right words to name the gulf inside of me and the sickly yellow light that floods my vision every time I pass the train station. So instead, I tell him I am okay, or fine, or tired, and I fall deeper into the Chasm.

I wonder how long it will be before he falls out of love with me, and I wonder if it will be before or after the wedding.

But for now, as I keep vigil beside my halmoni, he wakes me up every morning with a video of our dogs and tells me he loves me and misses me and hopes I am sleeping enough and not working too hard. He sends my parents a Christmas card written in Korean and promises to call on New Year's Day, Seoul time, to bow to my parents in the Korean custom. He claps when I play the cello for him, and he props the phone up on the piano so he can play me a fugue.

And I wonder, perhaps, if my memory turned him into the villain I needed to appease my own guilt—to believe B. abandoned me in my time of need, rather than face how I abandoned my brother. I remember, over and over, that B. didn't take the next flight back to New York after I told him about the accident. But don't I also remember that he did *try* get the next flight out? And when he couldn't, didn't I instruct him not to cut his trip short? Didn't he wander for miles (or kilometers) in the wild mountains, desperately looking for a signal so he could call me? Didn't he tell me that he would do everything I asked, and beg me to tell him anything I needed? Didn't he reach deep into the folds of his own grief and memory to tell me what it was like for him in the immediate wake of his father's suicide? How guilty he felt that his last conversation with his father was one of annoyance that their phone lines were about to be shut off? That I wasn't a piece of shit for only half listening to my brother the night he was hit? How my shock and grief and despair were entirely expected and that I was not alone?

I wonder why I could hear Mentor and the Senior as they spoke the same words to me, but I could not hear B. And I wonder at the patience of this man who has stayed beside me through my descent into madness.

I wonder if maybe the bronze anvil has ceased falling, and whether his boundless optimism is the lyre that might wrench me from the under-gloom.

99 Pounds

My halmoni decides to eat just enough every four days or so to give us hope, and then goes back to refusing to swallow. She spends a good amount of the day examining her bear, playing with its ribbon, looking at it this way and that, and sometimes trying to tear apart her pillow.

She goes days without responding, except when I try to take the bear. She shakes her head, no, you cannot have it, give it back.

But she doesn't answer me anymore when I ask her how she is, or what her name is, or who I am.

She will only move her lips now when we try to sing with her. No voice. It doesn't help that I only know the English words to the songs, and she only knows the Korean.

Grandma tries to get her to sing along to hymns they used to sing together, and I play the melodies on my mother's cello between practicing Elgar. (I remember when we were still living in New Jersey, my halmoni picked up my bow and thought it was a bow for archery and pretended to shoot an arrow. I laughed as my mother explained to her that this was a totally different type of bow.)

We give her the IV drip every day through a needle in her ankle, and each time she tries to raise her foot, I pull it back down. I think she begins raising her foot more and more because I won't let her.

She won't respond if I call out to her, and sometimes she will only stare in one direction. She never fails to respond to the bear, though, and it becomes my main mode of communication with her.

"Halmoni, isn't this bear cute?"

"Yes, it is very cute." Her answer is barely a whisper.

"Where did you get it?"

"I bought it."

"Where?"

"I bought it. At a department store."

"What is it?"

"It is my baby."

"You bought your baby?"

"At a department store."

Or sometimes it is a cat. Or just an object. It never has a name. She agrees that we should give it a name, but does not offer one.

My dad asks me how long I think she will live. I have no answer, so instead I ask him whether he thinks it will be okay for the aunts to come in February. He shrugs. My mom thinks yes.

"If she stops eating entirely, will you keep her on the IV?"

"I don't know. Who are we doing this for? It's up to your dad and your aunts. But it would be a different story if she were totally gone. Once they see her, and see that she has these moments where she is awake, they won't be able to do it. It's not about logic."

I stroke my halmoni's cheek and her hair when I sit beside her, and I wonder again if she knows somewhere inside that we are treating her like a baby. I don't know why we are keeping her alive, and I don't know how we can do anything else.

Her cheeks are hard, which I had never noticed before. My mom says they have been like that forever. "She had cheek implants."

"When? That seems like a big surgery."

"It was before I got married."

"Really? I had no idea. I never noticed."

"I didn't know until a couple years ago. We were in a taxi coming back from church and she started having a seizure in the cab. I tried to hold her face in my hands and her cheeks were hard. I started crying, I was so shocked. I thought she was dead and what is that called, rigor?"

"Rigor mortis?"

"Yeah. I thought her body was already stiff."

"Rigor mortis takes hours to set in, you know."

"You don't think about that in the moment! So here I am screaming and crying and the driver takes us to the hospital and it was only a small seizure. Not good, obviously, but not rigor mortis. I was so mad that no one told me about her cheeks. Because you kiss your mother-in-law on the cheek, but you don't really ever grab her cheeks, so how would I have known? Stop laughing!"

"It's funny!"

"It wasn't funny when I was in the cab. Maybe it's a little funny now."

"I wonder why she got cheek implants."

"Does the drip look done? I should close it so no air gets in."

Grandma touches my halmoni's leg. "She's getting so skinny."

My halmoni looks at me and smiles when I smile. Then she goes back to her bear.

백두산

It is New Year's Eve. At lunch, my dad pours us all a glass of 백세주, an herbal rice liquor that is supposed to help you live to be a hundred.

"There was a boy who toasted his grandmother at her hundredth birthday with 백세주 and said, 'May you live to be a hundred years old!'"

My parents laugh. My dad looks happy and relaxed. My mom is busy trying to get her mother not to push her food onto my plate.

"엄마, there is plenty of food, you have to eat all of that."

"It's too much!"

"엄마!"

"Okay, okay."

They drink and eat and appear normal. At ease.

I don't know how to live in this reality. My mother must be as dead inside as I am, but I don't want to make her cry so I say nothing and I laugh with them. I conjure the image of my brother, that happy boy, and push it away hurriedly, worried that my glutamate receptors will break down. I wonder what it's like to live in my halmoni's head, in a past where my brother is still alive. I wonder if she knows, somewhere in there, that the past is not present.

I wonder if, once my halmoni goes, my mother will be free.

We open a bottle of champagne at dinner because everyone will be asleep by midnight. We hand my halmoni a glass for the toast, and she refuses to give it back to my mother. My mother helps her bring the cup to her lips, and she swallows a sip.

"She won't drink water, but she'll drink champagne."

After dinner, we wheel her to the living room and my dad plays Nina Simone. I have just introduced him to the song Sinnerman, which he cannot stop playing. He begins telling me trivia about her life and I laugh and tell him that I, too, have read Nina Simone's Wikipedia page.

When my halmoni begins to fall asleep, I wheel her to her room. She is wide awake once we get there and doesn't want to get into bed, so I play the Korean national anthem for her on the cello, and she mouths some of the words. I also play Auld Lang Syne, which was the melody we used for the anthem before we wrote our own melody. She doesn't sing along to that, but she smiles at me.

I don't remember when I became part of the Korean We. I will lose this when she is lost and gone forever, when I no longer have anything pulling me back to this beautiful, hazy, suffocating, free land of the morning calm.

동해물과 백두산이 마르고 닳도록
하나님이 보우하사 우리나라 만세
무궁화 삼천리 화려강산
대한 사람 대한으로 길이 보전하세

"사랑해요. I love you."

She looks directly into my eyes with complete clarity as she answers: "나도, I love you."

I kiss her forehead and she loses focus again. I leave before she can see me sob.

January 1. Happy New Year!

I am still sleeping when B. calls to pay his respects.

"Sleepyhead."

I blearily show him to my parents and grandmothers and tell him I love him and that I'll see him next year, since New York is still in the past.

For the first time in twenty years, my dad insists that we all wear 한복 for New Year's Day bows. My mother puts me in her own yellow 한복, which looks absurd on me but fits just well enough that I will be able to bow.

"Take a video of us so we can share with the family. Everybody will be happy to see her."

My parents bow to my halmoni first. "새해복많이 받으세요."

They kiss her on the cheek and ask which of them looks nicer. She doesn't respond and looks at her bear instead.

It is my turn.

I bow alone.

"새해복많이 받으세요. Happy New Year."

"Happy New Year," she whispers to me in English. She puts a beaded bracelet over my wrist, a trinket of green and red plastic that she made years ago at the senior center, and which has sparkled majestically on her shelf ever since.

My parents rush over when they see her respond.

"Happy New Year!"

"Happy New Year," she whispers again.

My parents bow to my grandma next.

"I didn't prepare any envelopes . . ."

"엄마, I told you we aren't doing money this year."

She blesses them both and cries a little bit.

It is my turn.

I remember the last photograph I have of my grandpa before he became sick: my brother and me bowing to my grandpa and my grandma.

Only grandma and me left now from that image. I bow to her and she hugs me.

My parents take their places to receive my bow. They touch my head in blessing and kiss me on the cheek.

"Okay, let's eat."

We eat rice cake soup while my halmoni watches us and plays with her bear.

Thirty days since I was called home and somehow she is still alive, or at least her heart continues to beat.

My theory is, if you go thirty days wanting to kill yourself . . .

These rare moments in which the veil lifts and she sees us through her haze—do we bring her back here?

Does she want to come back?

32 Years (Flash Forward)

She went in her sleep.

Like last time, she hadn't been eating. Like last time, I had flown home on a whim, a month after I turned thirty-two.

Unlike last time, I flew in the middle of a global pandemic. I wore two masks during the fourteen-hour flight and was detained in a government facility upon arrival for having a temperature of 0.3 degrees above regulation.

When I was released and arrived home, I was quarantined from the rest of the house through a plastic sheet and a glass door. My grandma left food out for me on the dining table. I ate alone and waved at her through the glass.

When I was sure I wasn't incubating a deadly plague, I went to see my halmoni. She had no words for me, but she smiled when she saw me. Once, she waved. I showed her pictures of B. and me from our wedding. He is wearing a navy, silk-lined tuxedo, and I am in a white silk dress that sweeps out around my waist and floats above the ground. Gossamer wings flutter down from my shoulders and form a translucent cape behind me. I have no veil and instead wear a tiara shaped in flowers and vines. In another picture, we have both changed into 한복 (B. in a cobalt blue vest lined in cream, with dark silk trousers, and me in a sky blue silk skirt and a cream top with a pale pink sash and peach-colored chrysanthemums embroidered on my sleeves), and we are laughing at our dogs, who are dressed in tuxedos.

My halmoni patted me on the back of my hand.

I could lift her up in my arms if I wanted. She was nothing but bones and skin and a beautiful head of silver hair. Every morning and every night, my dad came into the room and spoke to her. When he was in the room, she would look at no one else.

One Saturday, my dad went to the gym and to pick up his belated birthday cake. In the meantime, we tried to feed my halmoni squash porridge, but she was too sleepy to swallow, so my mother used a syringe, and then her finger, to remove all the porridge from her mouth so she wouldn't choke in her sleep.

She dozed all morning, and then she didn't.

She was still warm when we came back into the room. So warm that my mother and I looked frantically for signs of life for almost an hour.

Is the pulse I feel at her wrist through my thumbs hers, or my own?

"She is gone, I think."

I call my dad and say only, "Can you come home?"

"Okay." He hangs up without another word.

My mother keeps putting her finger under my halmoni's nose, but feels no breath. She is sobbing and my halmoni's flowery purple pajamas are becoming soaked with tears.

Did she speak in her last moments? Why weren't we with her? I see a tear in the corner of her right eye, which died closed.

Grandma comes in and sees her and begins to wail.

My dad comes home and puts his arm around my mother and me. He speaks soft words to my mother. About how well she cared for his mother. About how no one could have done better. My mother continues to spill tears.

But I am not there. Tears are running down my cheeks, but all I can wonder is if she is free. If my mother is free. If my father is free.

My dad deals with the morgue while my mother's mother, my mother, and I change his mother's clothes. We strip her of her pajamas and change her underwear.

She is still warm. Her skin is soft and almost young in its smooth luster, stretched over shrunken bones. I show my mother the photograph I took of my halmoni years ago, in the garden, wearing her gray and purple silk 한복. The death portrait she commissioned from me while she was yet living.

My mother pulls out that same dress. We carefully pull the white silk undergarments over her legs. We pull her thin arms through the top loops of the shimmering violet skirt, which hangs on her shoulders like an apron, and which we wrap around her body. I lift her so that we can fold the silk around her. Still warm. We pull her arms through the light gray sleeves of the top, and my mom carefully ties the dark red sash in a traditional bow.

"Take a picture of her. She looks like she is sleeping."

I do, although she doesn't. She looks like she has died.

My mother has somehow found a large color print of the picture I showed her, which I must have sent to her the last time we thought halmoni would go.

The mortician comes and bears the body away. My father and my mother go with him. They return with a box wrapped in silk, a picture framed in gold, and a birthday cake. My father combines her ashes with the ashes of his father he brought home those years ago.

"They are together again after forty-eight years."

My dad gives us each a slice of cake as Nina Simone plays in the background.

"With sadness and relief that my mother no longer has to endure a less than perfect life, I want to gather our thoughts for her."

He turns to me. "Maybe you can write them down. About 멍멍이, too. So that we remember even the little things about them."

Muse, sing.

And I begin:

Once upon a time . . .

Notes

Once upon a time . . . The start of narrator's story, which she hears from her halmoni and passes on to her brother. The O in Once also stands in for Chapter Zero, a prologue.

I, being of unsound mind and body. Roman numeral I, and I indicating herself. A draft will and a dramatis personae.

To Remember, I Write. To, a homonym for 2.

Three Nights. The third night is when she was taken to the doctor.

Brodmann Area (BA) 44/45. Brodmann Areas 44 and 45 make up Broca's Area, which controls language.

Quincunx. The five dots on a die.

Six Sentences. Six-sentence exercise.

子. 홍옥선, maiden name 장. 子 is the character for Rat in Chinese Astrology. It looks like a 7.

BA 8. Blind Spot. BA for frontal eye field and uncertainty.

For Nine Nights and Days . . . Continuation of narrator's story about Orpheus and Eurydice.

BA 10. I remember. BA for memory recall.

November 17. A date she does not want to remember.

Every night for twelve years . . . Continuation of narrator's story about Eurydice and Orpheus.

13 조선 Ships. Battle of Myeongyang.

14 Enigma Variations. By Elgar.

'15. Leaving Elba. Napoleon escaped from exile on Elba in 1815.

16 Hours. 5 a.m. to 9 p.m.

Line 17. Under the Harvest Moon. The last line (line 17) of the poem "Under the Harvest Moon," by Carl Sandburg, reads, "Beautiful, unanswerable questions."

1.8320128(17)×10−24 cal/°R. Boltzmann constant. Appears in entropy formulae.

1-978. Andover Parents' Weekend. 978 is the area code for Andover, MA.

20. The Resistance. Korean age of her grandma's grandfather when he went abroad.

To One, a Pinhole. To One is a homonym for Two-One. Twenty-one is also narrator's age in the dialogue.

22.08.1862 (Doctor) Gradus ad Parnassum. Birthdate of Claude Debussy.

23 Pairs of Chromosomes. Self-explanatory.

24. On a scale of 1–10, what face do you feel? Narrator sits by her grandfather's bedside for twenty-four hours before leaving to move the car.

25. The American Dream. Her halmoni came to this country with twenty-five dollars.

26. Fe (Iron). 26 is the atomic number for iron.

For nine hours, and nine more, and nine more . . . End of narrator's story of Orpheus and Eurydice.

28. Remember. Narrator tells a story of when her cousin spent twenty-eight weeks in a Korean daycare.

Messier 29 . . . A star cluster in the constellation Cygnus.

Flash Forward: 30 Days. A glimpse of a future conversation with Mentor, and a running theme throughout: Mentor tells narrator that one may kill oneself if one goes thirty straight days with no reprieve from wanting to die.

Bed 31. Chris's bed number in the hospital.

Flash Forward: 32 Years. A glimpse of the future. Narrator is thirty-two years old when her halmoni finally dies, but this does not happen until later.

33. Elohim. Promises of God. Jesus dies at age thirty-three.

No. 34. Attendre et espérer. In the *Count of Monte Cristo* by Alexandre Dumas (père), Edmond Dantès is imprisoned in cell No. 34. A theme of the novel is: "Toute la sagesse humaine sera dans ces deux mots: *attendre et espérer*!"

35,904' 청계천. Approximate length of the river in feet.

Incident Report #36030 (Six More Sentences). The incident report of narrator's collapse against the tree and admission to the psychiatric emergency ward.

BA 37. Death Mask. BA of language association, visual perception, and extended Wernicke's area (brain region for language development).

38th Parallel. Remember . . . ? The division point of North and South Korea.

3:09 a.m. February (When). Narrator's admission time into the hospital.

Messier 40 . . . is an optical double star in the constellation Ursa Major.

1-401. Sunday Morning. 401 is the area code mentioned in the chapter.

The Answer to Life, the Universe, and Everything is 42 (see *Hitchhiker's Guide to the Galaxy* by Douglas Adams).

4:3. Ennui/Offui. 4:3 is a standard television aspect ratio.

44. Shade. Tetraphobia is common in Korea, and the number four is often associated with death.

4.5 stitches per inch. Knitting gauge.

BA 46. Phantom Limb. Theorized as an area related to phantom limb pain.

Some limited success treating this area for depression using transcranial magnetic stimulation.

4? 7? Narrator's guesses at a pain scale of one to ten.

48. Cadmium. 48 is the atomic number for cadmium, which is used as a control rod to manage the fission rate of plutonium/uranium. See also *Copenhagen* by Michael Frayn.

Dwelt a miner forty-niner and his daughter Clementine. From the song *My Darling Clementine*, which narrator and her halmoni sing. Also calls to mind Clementine from the movie *Eternal Sunshine of the Spotless Mind*, another story of memory loss.

50 Righteous People. See Genesis 18:24.

+51. Direct Dial to Psychiatric Emergency. Intra-building number for psychiatric emergency ward.

52 People Long. The ward list is fifty-two people long.

53. Iodine. 53 is the atomic number for iodine, a disinfectant.

Six by Nine (Not the Answer to Life, the Universe, and Everything). 6 x 9 = 54, but it also equals 42 in base 13. This is the anti-answer; the question, but the wrong question.

Five by Five. Code for all good, loud and clear.

Messier 56. Swan Song of a Lyre. Star cluster in the constellation Lyra, between the Cygnus beta and the Lyra gamma.

Messier 57. Ring Nebula. A ring nebula in the constellation Lyra.

58 Weeks Later // A Memorial to Young Womanhood (or The Spirit of Youth). 58 weeks after what happened to her in February. The subtitle is the name of a sculpture along the path she walks.

BA 5/9. Darkness Visible. BA 5 is for working memory, pain, and saccade. BA 9 is for memory and potentially religion. *Darkness Visible* is a reference to William Styron's memoir of his depression and recovery.

Boethius says history is a wheel.

6.0 Sentences, Again. The six-sentence prompt, this time about M.

June 11, 4:Something AM. The date of the car crash.

6:20 a.m. The first morning in the hospital.

6:30 p.m. The first evening in the hospital.

64. Gadolinium Contrast Media. 64 is the atomic number of gadolinium, which is used for contrast dyes for MRIs.

Messier 65. Spiral Galaxy in Leo. Messier 65 is an intermediate spiral galaxy in the constellation Leo, the lion.

June 6, 1987: D-Day. Narrator's parents' wedding anniversary.

*67. If youre [sic] reading this, its [sic] too late. Reference to the title of a Drake album, which also has a song titled *Star67*.

68. Greenberg 2 South West. Weill Cornell Hospital is on 68th Street and York Avenue in Manhattan. Greenberg 2SW is the neuro ward.

69. June 21–July 22. The astrological sign and date range for Cancer.

Lucky Number 7. M.'s lucky number.

July 14. M.'s birthday. Bastille Day.

72 Days After the Accident. Self-explanatory.

73rd and Broadway. The site of the accident.

74 Days Later (Thanksgiving). Seventy-four days after B.'s proposal to narrator.

Unit 7, 5 Peter Cooper Village. An apartment where narrator used to live.

76th and Broadway. The cross-street of the apartment narrator shared with M.

7/11. American Dream, Redux. M. really liked 7/11 Slurpees.

78. Shneim Asar Chodesh. The text references seventy-eight municipalities about to go bankrupt. Shneim Asar Chodesh is the Jewish mourning period for a parent.

Lil Chano from 79th. A nickname for Chance the Rapper.

∞. Time Travel. The infinity sign is an eight tipped over.

8 Months, 10 Days. February (Entropy). 8 months and 10 days after the accident was in February, and on narrator's father's birthday.

February 28. Greenberg 14 South. 28 is an inversion of 82 (the number of this chapter). Greenberg 14S is the new hospice ward.

Messier 83. Spiral Galaxy in Hydra. Messier 83 is a spiral galaxy in the constellation Hydra and near the constellation Cancer. Hydra and Cancer are referenced elsewhere in the myth of Heracles. Narrator spirals in her head and spirals around Iceland.

TI-84. Where There's Not a Will. A TI-84 is a graphing calculator.

85. ἄστατος. 85 is the atomic number of astatine, a rare and unstable element. The name derives from the Greek word for "unstable" or "disordered."

Eighty-Sixed. Eighty-sixed means nixed, no longer available.

Messier 87. Supermassive Black Hole. Messier 87 is a supermassive black hole, and the first to be photographed.

88. Constellations. The International Astronomical Union recognizes eighty-eight constellations. Eighty-eight is also a lucky number in some Asian cultures.

1989–???. Narrator's birth to an unknown future, and the span between.

90. In Ruth Bader Ginseng's name we pray, a(wo)man. Her halmoni turns ninety.

91 Wedding Guests. They send out ninety-one save-the-date cards.

92. Merry-Go-Round. Her halmoni is ninety-two years old when she visits.

93. 홍자범. She wonders if her halmoni will see the age of ninety-three, and realizes that her halmoni already is ninety-three in Korean age.

94. Plutonium. 94 is the atomic number for plutonium.

I-95. New York to Boston. I-95 is the main highway between New York and Boston.

96th Street. Where she originally considered buying an apartment.

1997. First Woman President. 1997 is the year the first woman took office as Secretary of State in the United States.

9.8 m/s². The acceleration of gravity.

99 Pounds. The weight of her halmoni when she stops eating.

백두산. Baekdu Mountain, a sacred mountain mentioned in the Korean national anthem. Baek means white in this context, but is also the word for one hundred.

January 1. Happy New Year! January 1 is 1/01.

32 Years (Flash Forward). Narrator's age when her halmoni dies, and chronologically the last event of the story.

Acknowledgments

To Kate Gale, Rebeccah Sanhueza, Aimee Lu, and everyone at Red Hen Press: Thank you for understanding my story and bringing it to life. I couldn't imagine working with better people.

To Liv Albert: You are an incredible inspiration in bringing mythology to the masses without losing nuance and rigor. I can't thank you enough for reading this book without even knowing me.

To Helen Wan: Your work on diversity in the law, both in fiction and in life, helped me feel less alone. I'm grateful to you for being so open, genuine, and friendly in response to my cold email.

To Raza: You have been a friend like no other, and the purveyor of a salad that changed my life.

To Jordi: You inspired me to write, and you inspired me to become a lawyer, and you inspire me every day to be patient and level-headed.

To Juri: You told me once that I was your black swan event. You were certainly mine, and without you, this book and my brain do not exist.

To Milquelia: What would my life be if I hadn't met you in that kitchen all those years ago? (Empty, joyless, bereft of potato salad.)

To Katherine: No one has ever benefited so much from you yelling at the Dominican president as I have. I'm so glad that's the way we met.

To Sonia: You were the first person ever to read an early version of this and make me believe it could live somewhere outside of my head. Your workshop notes have made this book better than I believed possible.

To Dianisbeth: Your unwavering support has given me life in these past few years. Without you, this book would be obscure and formless, with too much science.

To Rachel: Sorry to Daniel, but he knows you are the other half of my brain. Without you, I do not exist.

To Daniel: I love you. I aspire to your optimism and I live on your unwavering support.

To 외할머니: 사랑해요!

To Umma and Appa: This family is built on all that you gave us. Thank you for everything, and most of all for your love. I love you more than life itself.

Biographical Note

Eunice Hong is the director of the Davis Polk Leadership Initiative at Columbia Law School. She was previously a litigation associate at Paul, Weiss, Rifkind, Wharton & Garrison LLP and a law clerk to the Honorable Richard M. Berman in the United States District Court for the Southern District of New York. Her debut novel, *Memento Mori*, is the winner of the 2021 Red Hen Press Fiction Award. *Memento Mori* was also on the 2021 Dzanc Prize for Fiction Longlist, a 2021 UNO Press LAB Semifinalist, and a 2019 Louise Meriwether First Book Prize Finalist. Eunice received her undergraduate degree from Brown University and her JD from Columbia Law School. She resides in New York City, New York, with her husband and two dogs.

Printed in the USA
CPSIA information can be obtained
at www.ICGtesting.com
JSHW020348150324
59192JS00004B/20